D1045703

YOU CAN'T UNSCRAMBLE
THE OMELET

A Novella

VICKI SOLÁ

Perswayssick Press & Audio Works LLC

Cover designed by Jay Hudson
(www.yojayhudson.com)
Cover Illustration Copyright © 2019 by Jay Hudson

Vicki Solá
Visit my website at www.gneeecey.com

Published in the United States of America by
Perswayssick Press & Audio Works LLC
New Milford, New Jersey

ISBN-978-0-9600031-0-5 – E-book
ISBN-978-0-9600031-1-2 – Paperback

Library of Congress Control Number: 2019902652

Author photo: Vicki Solá. Photo credit: Roberto Vasquez, 2013

Colophon by Jay Hudson

For
Hedda Solá-Westhead and Audrey Grossman,
who make the heavens shine a little brighter.

FOREWORD

So here I aaam, *meee*, The Grate One, Diroctor Bizzig Gneeecey, writin' this lousy foreword. Better than a backward. Wasn't *asked* to write it, just kinda barged in an' forced my way. (As usual). But I *do* igspect to get paid.

This hapoopens to be that Earth human Vicki Solá's second book 'bout me. (The firs' one she stooopidly titled *The Getaway That Got Away*). Guess she jus' can't leave a good thing alone. An' true to form, most of what's in here's a buncha untrue false lies.

Jus' sayin'. To make matters worse, my attorney John Smiff, Equestrian, may not be able to pursue interdimensional legal action 'gainst her. Also, she did not heed my brilliant legal advice to add the followin' stinkin' disclaimer: "Annny similarities to persons livin' or dead are purely coincidental. All names have been changed."

An' one mo' thang. The lousy title, *You Can't Unscramble the Omelet*, is somethin' *I* once said. So, if this book does go viral or whatever you carbonated Earth life-forms call it, I do *fully* igspect to get a percentage of that too. (The money, not the disease).

—Diroctor B.Z.Z. Gneeecey
St. Bogelthorpe Park, TheOtherRealNewJersey
Decvembruary 42, 32609x

"Vicki Solá knows how to tell a story."

-1-

IG'S GOT A NEW ROOMIE

SPRING. NEVER THOUGHT it would arrive.

One hand on my faux leather-covered steering wheel, I wound my window down, savoring the sweet scents of cherry blossoms as they mingled with those of the piping-hot Cuban coffee and steaming buttered blueberry-orange muffin (gluten-free, of course) that I'd just picked up at Javier's Deli.

An almost summery breeze swept through my blonde-dyed hair, pleasing me, as did the sight of my sleek red '64-and-a-half Mustang, reflected in Main Street's store windows. My late dad had done a meticulous job restoring the car—his last gift to me. Couldn't believe it had already been seven years since I'd graduated from high school. I clicked the knob on my ancient CD player and cranked up the volume. Better watch out, I thought, chuckling as I bopped to the heavy-duty, percussion-driven salsa music blaring from my speakers. I, Nicki Rodriguez, might get busted for dancing in my car. My almost-boyfriend, bandleader Carlos Santiago, had really outdone himself with this new production. There was already talk of a Grammy nomination.

Smiling, I pictured the green-eyed, well-built six-footer. I reached for my muffin, then glanced up to see the head of a white-and-black canine-humanoid rise in my rearview mirror.

"Keep on driving!" it shrieked.

I fell out of bed and woke up.

✻ ✻ ✻

CLUTCHING MY INJURED HIP and rubbing what felt like a cracked cranium, I staggered into the kitchen, my basement apartment's gray cement tiles sending shockwaves through the soles of my bare feet. If not for the carpet beneath my bed, thin and cheap as it was, I might've been wiping my addled brains off the floor.

I smacked the light switch and squinted.

Three a.m. read the cat-with-the-wagging-tail clock nailed up on the brick wall. It appeared to be watching my every move.

"We've gotta stop meeting like this, Ms. Kitty," I muttered, snatching my ugly poop-brown WUGG-FM Radio mug from the dish drain—the porcelain piece of junk my pain-in-the-culo boss Bill Fernández had forced me to take home.

Tea...tea...had to make a cup of chamomile. Couldn't stand something about its taste, but at least it might help me fall asleep again. Thought only old people woke up in the wee hours and couldn't get back to sleep. Ain't supposed to happen when you're twenty-five.

Not that I didn't have the kind of problems that would keep you awake. Only trouble was, I couldn't tell you what half of 'em were. Yeah, there were the usual ones, like my horrible full-time job at that New York

Spanish commercial radio station. I stared up at the low beige ceiling, with its maze of half-painted hanging pipes.

And there were all the freakin' bills piled up on my dad's old mahogany desk. Constant car repairs, too many credit cards, student loans. Most still unpaid. My freelance recording business, NickelRod Productions, was supposed to close the gap *and* allow me to eat, in theory. But, oh, the clients...obnoxious...and so resistant to paying. I needed to be a collection agency too. I shivered, partly from the chill in the air and partly from the horror, as my life floated past like a bad movie on that giant silver screen inside my head.

The stuff that I couldn't remember troubled me the most. Carlos was losing patience with me. He couldn't understand why my sad face. He had even asked if there was someone else. A slight remembrance of someone else, somewhere else, troubled me. Often.

In a couple of weeks, I was to jet off to Paris for five whole days, where I'd emcee Carlos' salsa band in several exclusive nightclubs. Springtime in Paris.

Sighing, tea unmade, I ambled into my living room/office, plopped into my high-backed black pleather chair and pulled the chain on my grandma Isabel's antique brass lamp. I studied my right hand under the golden light, still puzzled by my skin's lavender tinge.

Suddenly, someone was knocking on my door. Vigorously. I almost jumped through the ceiling, half-painted pipes and all. Who was out there banging at this time of night—or more accurately, *morning*? "I'm not gonna answer," I half-whispered, bolting out of my chair and flying back into the kitchen, then skidding to a stop.

Lost for words, I stared up the stairs at the silvery steel door as it appeared to unlatch and open itself.

Framed in the doorway stood a white-and-black canine-humanoid, a smug smirk plastered across his grungy face. He clutched a clipboard in one cartoonish four-fingered hand, and what appeared to be a purple rubber briefcase in the other. He wore a propeller-topped chrome yellow civil defense helmet, a sloppy giant black letter "F" painted on the front. A small gold hoop glistened from his left ear.

"Bad mornin', Ig," he squealed, slamming the door and skipping down the steps. When he dropped his purple bag at my feet, it bounced. Twice.

My lips parted, but my vocal cords were on strike. He followed me as I hobbled back into the other room. Entire body enveloped by a prickly sensation, I lowered myself into my big chair. Maybe it was just another bad dream.

"Well, Ig, ain'cha hapoopy to see me? I certaincerely hope ya are!" His bulging yet beady eyeballs remained riveted on me.

Embarrassed sitting there in my pajamas, (the gray flannel ones with the Dalmatian pups driving fire engines), I sprang up and sprinted into my bedroom to pull on my old scarlet bathrobe, the one with the torn pocket. I tied the belt around my ever-shrinking waist as I trotted back to my desk, energized by a prolonged surge of adrenaline.

"I mean," the creature continued in his shrill, nerdy voice, twirling his helmet propeller, "wasn'cha worried 'bout me after that invisible force, y'know, sepooparated us when we got stuck in that weird dimension wit' all them ice crystals, where we didn't know which way was up or if we'd ever get home or ever see each other again? Huh, Ig, huh?"

"Name's *Nicki*," I managed to croak. "*Nicki Rodriguez.*"

"I know, Ig. I know." The elbow-high entity shifted from long narrow foot to long narrow foot as my tired eyes bored into his.

"Actually," I added, as memories came flooding back, "I was really worried about where you ended up, and what happened to you…after that mysterious force tore us apart…*separated* us."

Chest puffed out, he grinned.

I folded my arms. "Well, what're you doing here? At three o'clock in the morning? And how did you get in? That door up there was locked."

"Questions, questions, Ig."

"Well?"

He tossed his clipboard at my paper-covered desk, knocking a tower of bills down onto the cobalt blue rug. "*Yooou* opened the door, ya Ig."

"I did not."

"Ya did too!"

My eyes narrowed. "Did not. *Would* not."

"I couldn't. My two stinkin' hands were holdin' junk."

It was true. Both his fuzzy mitts had been full. My legs went weak, but my voice grew stronger. "Well, what are you doing here? In *my* apartment?"

"Oxidatin'. Y'know, breathin'. Respoopiratin'. Heh hah, heh haah, heh haaah!"

Hapoopy. Sepooparated. Respoopiratin'. I shook my head. It was all coming back to me. He still suffered from ooglitis, a speech impediment caused by exposure to mierk, a toxic, goopy brown substance that blighted his otherworldly dimension of Perswayssick County. And enriched a select few individuals. "Answer my question, Doctor Gneeecey."

He whisked his clipboard off my desk, spilling more papers. "That's *Diroctor* Gneeecey. Pronouced 'Guh-neeecey,' wit' a hard G. An' perhaphoops ya don't rememboober, I'm a doctor *plus* I'm stinkin' director of Perswayssick County. That makes me a stinkin' *diroctor.*"

I grunted.

"An' of course, ya mus' rememboober that I'm a self-made zillionaire! Own lotsa consonants. An' vowels!"

My jaw muscles began to twitch. "Diroctor, I want an answer. What are you doing here in *my* neck of the universe? *Again?*"

"I think ya know the answer to *that,* Iggy Rockhead."

Scowling, I crumpled a blank NickelRod invoice and flung it at Gneeecey's oversized head. And missed. "Told you before. Name's Nicki Rodriguez—actually, Nicole Rodriguez."

"Stinkin' whatever."

"Now answer my question."

He stomped his red high top sneakered foot. "I'm here 'cause ya got somethin' that's *mine*."

I crouched down and began scooping my bills off the carpet. "What could I possibly have that's yours?"

Gneeecey marched into my bedroom, as if he was familiar with the place, and yanked open my pine dresser's deep bottom drawer.

Fists clenched, I ran in after him. "Who said you could go in there?"

"Yammicles! I *knowed* she had ya!" Dark eyes darting my way, he lifted out a limp brown teddy bear by the neck. A singed greenback protruded from its torn, pouting muzzle.

Chills ran through me. I had forgotten entirely about the stuffed animal.

"An' looky," he shrieked, "there's my lousy thousan' dollar bill! It was missin' when I was countin' my stinkin' mon-ney this mornin'! Ya stole my bear *an'* my mon-ney!"

He pronounced the word money in such a nerdy way.

"I didn't steal anything! I remember now, you tied your bear Yammicles around my leg like a tourniquet when it was bleeding, when we were floating around in those ice crystals! I didn't steal anything!"

"Yammy," he continued, ignoring me, "ya okay? Obvooviously, she ain't been feedin' ya! Did she hurt'cha? Or make ya feel baaad? Or say anythin' baaad 'bout meee?"

"Diroctor Gneeecey, you've cornered the market on loopy."

"Says he's okay, Ig." Gneeecey trudged back to my desk. "Lucky for yo000u. If he wasn't, I woulda hadda made a snitizen's arrest! For endangerin' the welfare of a live stuffed bear!"

"Oh, puhlease." I had a bad taste in my mouth, and it wasn't from the tea I hadn't made. Suddenly an arrow shot through my solar plexus. "Do you think *they* followed you here?"

Gneeecey scratched his butt thoughtfully. "Hah?"

"You know, *them.*"

Gneeecey crammed the teddy into the bottomless pit of a pocket attached to his grimy aqua T-shirt. "Wha'cha talkin' 'bout, Ig? Who's them?"

I scuttled back into the kitchen and raced up the wooden steps, almost tripping on my long robe.

"Wha'cha doin', Ig?" he asked, waddling into the room.

"Bolting the door. I'm gonna ask you one more time. Do you think they followed you here?"

"Who? Ya got me totally mystificated, Ig. *Who* followed me?"

Exhausted, I gripped the banister as I made my way down the steep staircase. "*Them.* Those gangster pals of yours. Those floating eyeball creeps who cover themselves with that goopy poisonous mierk to create bodies for themselves. You know. Most of 'em even have the same name."

"Huh? Huh-an'-a-half?" Gneeecey shuffled back into the living room, right on my heels, invading my personal space. As usual.

My head turned. "C'mon, you know, the guys you owe all that money. The guys who tried to kill us several times?"

He ripped his civil defense propeller helmet off and threw it to the floor. "Oh, them. Y'mean Bob. An' Mark an' Mark. An' Mark, Mark an' Mark. An' Mark—"

"Cut the nonsense, Diroctor Gneeecey. Could they have followed you here?"

"Can't cut nonsense wit'out nonsense-cuttin' scissors, Ig," he replied, a sheepish expression spreading across his begrimed face. "Got any? Wit' them rounded points? Y'know, regoogoolar scissors can be priddy dangerousical. Specifoofically when ya run wit' 'em."

Reeling, I leaned against the wall and took a deep breath. "I'll ask you one more time. Do you think they followed you here? Into this dimension?"

"Dunno, Ig. Never thunk of it. But I do know I'm gonna hafta stay here wit' you for a while. Till my dimension burn lets up. Skin's all purpoople under my fur."

I pounded my fist on the desktop. "You can't stay here."

"I see your skin's still purpoople, too. I actually feel for ya, Ig. Never thought I'd say that. Dimension burn can be priddy horribooble."

"I appreciate your, uh, concern, Diroctor, but don't change the subject. You are not going to stay here."

"You stayed in my lousy mansion. For two whole stinkin' months!"

"Not because I wanted to. Had no choice, if you recall."

"Well, Ig, *this* sure ain't no mansion! I see that me an' Yammicles will be igstremely incornvenienced, stayin' here." Shooting me one of those 'Ain't this a dump?' looks, Gneeecey made a beeline back into my bedroom and flopped into my bed.

"Hey, get outta my—"

"You'll sleep on the floor, Ig," he ordered, sinking his head into my pillow.

I stood over him. "I said, get out of my bed."

"Ya proboobably forgot, I'm your boss."

My fists bunched up. "Not in this dimension, you're not!"

The canine-humanoid pulled my heavy maroon blanket and matching satin comforter over his pear-shaped body, sneakers and all.

A tall tumbler sparkled on the nightstand next to Gneeecey, catching my attention. The liquid inside had to be freezing cold. *Sure would love to dump that on the little jerk*, I thought, glancing down at him.

Fuzzy eyelids shut tight, a half-smile lighting his puss, he began to hum a doofy little tune.

At that moment, the vessel levitated and positioned itself directly over him.

My jaw dropped.

Tilting in midair, it poured its icy contents onto his noggin.

"Yaaaaaaaaaaaa!" Gneeecey leaped into the air and whacked his noodle on the rough-textured ceiling, just missing one of the pipes. "How daaare yooou?"

"I...I didn't do anything," I spluttered, wide-eyed, as the glass floated back to where it had been. "It...it...did it all by *itself*."

* * *

I POINTED TO THE OPEN bottom dresser drawer. "You're sleeping in there."

Gneeecey crawled in, fury flashing in his eyes. "C'mon, Yammy. I ain't seen no stinkin' sofa 'round here, jus' that big ol' stooopid desk, so ya gotta go back in that there lousy drawer. Can't igspect much hospoopitality from *her*. But this time, you'll be safe. You'll be wit' meee."

"Uh, Diroctor...aren't you gonna, you know, take your shoes off?"

Gneeecey looked at me like I had three freakin' heads. "Why, ya Ig?"

I threw him a fuzzy light blue blanket that, except for being clean, matched his T-shirt. "If you don't know, I really can't help you."

"Ya don't know much, do ya, Ig?"

"If you don't mind, Diroctor, *I* have to get up in the morning. Some of us have to *earn* our livings." I lowered myself onto my mattress and pulled the chain on my lamp.

Gneeecey yawned loudly. "Stinkin' whatever. Bad night, Ig."

"Yeah, freakin' whatever. Bad night," I replied, grudgingly returning his Planet Eccchs's customary evening salutation. I tossed my wet pillow onto the floor and stuffed the nearby dry one underneath my aching skull.

"Don't stinkin' say it like thaaat, so oogdimonious. Oh, an' by the way, Ig, another reason I'm here is that you still need to decipher them secret codes for me. The ones in that stooopid manuscript of yours. Y'know, in that weird book you're writin'."

"What?"

"Y'know, them secret codes you got that'll get me an' my fifteen million stranded snitizens of Perswayssick County back to our Planet Eccchs. Remembooober?"

"I told you last time I saw you, I have no freakin' idea what you're talking about. Now, go to sleep." Sighing, I rolled onto my stomach, pulled the covers up over my head and began to doze.

"Ig!"

My body went rigid. "What?" I growled into my pillow.

"You *are* gonna decipher them secret codes for me."

"Will you freakin' go to sleep?"

"Okay, Ig. We'll disgust this matter tomorrow. An' don'cha worry, me an' you are gonna have plenny of time together an'…"

Before he'd even finished his sentence, I'd begun dreaming. Something about a blizzard, and Bill Fernández calling me in to work. During my week off in July.

"*Ig! Ig! Ig!*"

Heart racing, I almost flew six feet up into the air. "*Whaf? Whaf? Whaf?*"

He moaned. "I caaan't sleep."

"*Now whaf?*"

"My *hand* hurts. From countin' all my mon-ney!"

"Will you freakin' shut up and go to sleep?"

-2-

HYPOOPNOTIZED

THE ALARM CLOCK'S SHRILL beep pierced my brain like a knitting needle dipped in acid. Five-thirty a.m.

Ugh. Had to make it to the radio station an hour earlier that morning to finish production on a bilingual commercial for a constipation remedy. For one of WUGG's newest clients—Grunts, Inc. I knew I could ace it and have the sixty-second spot ready to blast onto the airwaves in minutes. Only had to add the music bed and prerecorded flushing sounds. However, the micro-managing Bill Fernández, who wore a constant, pained expression of chronic constipation, wouldn't hear of me "leaving anything to chance." Even though the ad wasn't scheduled to air until after lunch.

Flinging off my covers, I swung my legs over the edge of the bed. As my frozen feet fished around for slippers, I glanced down at the open bottom dresser drawer. It was empty. What was Gneeecey doing up so early?

I grabbed my robe and raced toward the bathroom, turning on lights and stumbling over my hairy houseguest's helmet. Spotted my sleek new cellphone shimmering on a nearby bookshelf. Kept leaving the darned thing home.

As I entered the turquois-tiled privy, I flicked the switch and skidded to a stop. "*What the?*"

I squeezed my eyelids shut several times, but each time they opened, the mess was still there—yards and yards of wet toilet paper, plastered to the shower stall walls and beyond. "*Little creep.*" My words formed clouds in the frosty air as I sprinted into the kitchen.

There stood a drenched Gneeecey, sporting my pink paisley shower cap. Bits of toilet paper clung to his off-white snout and black triangular ears. "Bad mornin', Ig."

I pounded my fist on the round wooden tabletop. The good director blinked. I enunciated each word clearly. And loudly. "What...happened...in...the...bathroom?"

"Whaddaya mean, Ig?" he asked, wringing out the front of his sopping wet T-shirt over the dingy concrete floor.

"Don't 'Ig' me. There's toilet paper all over the walls in there. Must be a whole roll's worth."

"Oh, thaaat. Well, on the package, an' I used the last roll, it *said* bath tissue."

"Since when did *you* ever start taking baths?"

Gneeecey pointed to Yammicles, huddled in a puddle under the staircase. A crumpled strand of toilet tissue covered the cross-eyed teddy's dome, like a bad toupee. "Me an' Yammy didn't take no stinkin' bath, ya Ig. How in Bogelthorpe's name could we? Ya ain't got no lousy tub."

I punched the table again, harder, hurting my hand. Gneeecey flinched. "Diroctor, you never took a shower in the two months I stayed in your mansion. In fact, you bragged you hadn't bathed in two years. Said you didn't even know how to work your complicated faucets."

Gneeecey ripped the plastic cap off his noodle and hurled it at me.

"You *do* remember what toilet paper is for," I ventured, gripped by a sudden migraine.

Eyes narrowed, he began stomping on the shower cap. His deranged little dance was interrupted by a knock on the door—the one that led from my landlord's kitchen down into my apartment.

"Just a minute, Rico," I called up the stairs, suddenly hyperventilating. As I turned to Gneeecey, my voice morphed into a pleading whisper. "Diroctor, go back into the bedroom and stay there till I tell you it's okay to come out. *Please.*"

He kicked the shower cap under the table. "No."

"Do as I say," I ordered, shivering and perspiring at the same time.

Gneeecey grinned. "It's okay, Rico! C'mon down!"

"Sit—uh—lay down," I commanded the canine-humanoid. "And whatever you do, don't speak. You can bark, but don't—"

Ignoring me, Gneeecey extended a grubby white mitt. "Heya, Rico! Bad mornin'! Jack Russell's the name!"

"Rico Rosado," replied my thin, silver-haired landlord as he flew down the steps and grasped Gneeecey's hand. "Nice to meet'cha, Jack. *Encantado.*"

"I'm—I'm so sorry, Rico," I stammered as I glanced sideways at a sneering Gneeecey.

Rico's head tilted as he ripped a loose thread from his paint-splattered denim overalls.

"I mean, I never even asked you if I could keep a pet. Don't worry, this is just temporary. This dog's goin'!"

Rico's olive eyes grew huge. "Dog? Your friend here seems like a nice person."

"*Friend? He's not—*"

"Jack's cool. He can hang out here as long as he likes."

"But—"

"Nicki," continued Rico, pulling a wrench out of his back pocket, "I jus' wanted to find out when's a good time to come down an' fix your shower faucet. Probably jus' needs a washer to stop that annoyin' *an'* costly drippin'."

"Uh…uh…maybe later. After I come home from work—"

"Rico," interrupted Gneeecey, egg-shaped eyes gleaming, "ya can come down an' fix it anytime. *I'll* be here!"

✳ ✳ ✳

I SLAMMED A DISH under Gneeecey's fuzzy chin. "Here. Toast. Butter it yourself. Now, what's all this Jack Russell nonsense? And how come my usually sensible landlord thinks you're a regular person?"

The canine-humanoid held up both slices of burnt bread, eyeing them, and me, with disdain. Yammicles sat next to him, propped up on a folding chair, a white napkin tied bib-like around his worn plush neck. "I aaam a regoogoolar person. Don't understan' what in Bogelthorpe's name ya stinkin' mean."

I sat down beside him, lifted my coffee-filled WUGG mug and took a sip. This morning, the java smelled better than it tasted.

"Y'know, that's a real ugly mug, Ig. I mean that certaincerely."

"Diroctor, don't play games with me or try to change the subject. I don't have time. I have to go to work. Now, how come Rico sees you as a regular person, and not a, you know…"

"A stinkin' *whaaat?*"

My jaw tightened. "A dog. A walking, talking *dog.*"

Gneeecey dropped both pieces of toast back onto the apricot-colored plate and shoved it in front of Yammicles. "First, ya lousy Ig, I am not a dog. My dog Spot, back home, now he's a dog. But I am difooferent than you, uh, *humans*—thank Bogelthorpe for that." He paused. "More, y'know, advanced."

Clearing my throat, I glanced at my watch.

"An' by the way, Ig, me an' Yammy ain't eatin' this here lousy bread. It's on a cold plate, an' I saw on the package, it says gluten-free. *I* can *afford* gluten!"

"Found out a couple months ago that I have gluten sensitivity."

"Always knew you were weird, Ig."

"You're supposed to be a doctor, and I have to explain that having gluten sensitivity means I get sick if I ingest anything with wheat, barley, or rye?"

"Uh, us diroctors are busier than regoogoolar doctors. We don't got time to worry 'bout stuff that life forms like *you* might ingesticate."

I shook my head, remembering the mostly inedible items offered at his Gneeezle's Restaurant, back when I was stranded in his dimension of Perswayssick County. "And I'll have you know, Diroctor, just my luck, gluten-free foods cost *more*."

"I can stinkin' afford *that*, too!" He dug a knife into my non-dairy butter substitute and began gobbling it up, right out of the yellow plastic tub.

"Ugh—stop that! Gross! And stop always changing the subject. How come Rico thinks you're, uh, one of us?"

"I am one of us." He dipped a spoon into my new jar of marmalade, then jammed the overloaded utensil into his big pie hole. "I mean," he continued between annoying slurps, "you an' me, we're both here, so that makes us us." He licked his shiny black lips.

I grabbed the bottle and placed it out of his reach. "You know what I mean."

He lunged forward, seized the container and plunged a nearby fork into it. "Ya lousy Ig—"

"Nicki would be the name. And drop the 'lousy'."

"Stinkin' whatever, ya lousy Ig."

I tore the marmalade out of his hands again.

"Ain't polite to snatch stuff, Ig." He belched.

"Then don't take stuff. Now I asked you a question. And I expect an answer."

He began drinking from my thankfully almost empty carton of almond milk. "Well, Ig, seems *I*, Diroctor B.Z.Z. Gneeecey, also known as The Grate One, got the magical power to hypoopnotize youse Earth people." He smiled.

"Not me. You never did. And you never will."

He looked up thoughtfully, a milk mustache making his white fur appear even grimier. "Not yooou, 'cause ya met me on *my* turf when ya invaded my beautiful an' superior dimension. Ya stinkin' invaded my lousy Perswayssick County."

"Yeah, right."

"An' your milk sucks!"

"Don't change the subject again, Diroctor."

"I'm not. It does. Tastes real funny. But for some reason, I ain't laughin'."

I smashed my mug down on the table. The handle broke off and clunked to the floor.

"Look, Ig, ya busted your ugly cup."

"I'm gonna ask you one more time. Why did you tell Rico your name's Jack Russell?"

"Folks always whisper that name whenever I visit your mudball planet. I figure I mus' resembooble this Jack Russell guy. So, I use his name whenever I travel, y'know, incognizant to your dimension, which is quite frequent."

A chill ran down my spine.

"An' your coffee stinks, too," he added, admiring his reflection in a nearby glass. "Can't even eat it wit' a knife an' fork like I usually do—gotta drink it like soup! Disgustipatin'!" He adjusted his ears and smoothed down the hair on top of his head.

"Sorry. We don't have Merk Perk in our dimension. Us earthlings aren't into, uh, solid, bitter coffee. Oh, and when you have a chance, please pick up that helmet of yours. Put it in the closet. By the bedroom."

"Yeah. Stinkin' whatever. Later."

"Almost broke my neck on it this morning. And why's that black letter 'F' painted on it?"

"Well, Ig, I calcooculated mathemetratically that if every snitizen in Perswayssick County flushes their high-tech terlits at the same exac' time, it'll create enough force to catapult us stranded Planet Eccchsers back to our own dimension."

My eyes rolled up to the ceiling, then down to the cat-with-the-wagging-tail clock. If I didn't leave soon, I'd end up being late, despite having gotten up an hour earlier.

"So, ya Ig, the 'F' stands for Flush Day, my other plan I got in place 'cause I know I can't count on ya to come through wit' them secret codes." Picking his teeth, he shot me an icy glance.

I exhaled slowly.

"I'll tell ya more, Ig. Ya remboober my very igspensive terlit that only us rich people can afford—my Electronic Water Cyclone 3000?

Y'know, three-thousan' cyclones per flush an' it can also do your taxes plus ya can even vote from it?"

I rose. "Gotta go to work."

Gneeecey's face lit up.

"You lay low," I warned.

"Yeah. Stinkin' whatever." He removed an orange comb from his bulgy T-shirt pocket and began to style the short inky black fuzz that covered both sides of his head and dipped over his right eye. He ignored the crooked white channel of fur that ran from the top of his noggin and down the middle, to his bulbous honker.

Seized by a sudden burst of panic, I gasped. "Diroctor, do you have your, uh, meds with you? Hopefully, they're somewhere in your, uh, T-shirt pocket?"

He shrugged. "Hah?"

"Oh crap," I spluttered, "you know, your Bumpex and Repulsid, for your Redecoritis, and your, uh, *other* health issues?"

"Don't think I got 'em, Ig," he replied, groping around inside his lumpy pocket. "But that's okay. Ain't seen no dancin' trees or walkin' furniture since I been here. Although your dopey curtains were kinda starin' at me all funny a coupla minutes ago."

The knot in my stomach tightened. "What about your Millvill and your, uh, Health Cigars, for your, uh, you know, *problem*?"

The corners of his mouth turned upward.

"What about them, Diroctor?" My right foot began tapping, all by itself.

He shrugged. "Ain't got them neitherwise."

Acid rose up into my esophagus. "I'll call you at lunchtime. On my landline over there on the desk."

"Stinkin' whatever."

"And like I said, just stay quiet and lay low. And don't think you're calling the shots around here. This is *my* dimension." I kicked his purple rubber briefcase up against the wall. It bounced.

Gneeecey chuckled.

I started up the stairs, glaring back over my shoulder. "I expect to find you here, *alone*, when I return. And I expect to find this place *exactly* as it is."

-3-

NOT NOW, I'M WATCHIN' *OPRAH*

WHAT IS THIS?" demanded Bill Fernández as he scrambled into Production Studio A, waving his smartphone. "You even sent this—this picture—to my boss! And to her boss!" Jaw muscles twitching, my employer thrust his pricey device into my hands.

My face burned as I viewed the high-def image on the large screen, sent from my number, a selfie Gneeecey took sitting on my toilet, grinning the stupidest grin this side of the universe, orange-and-purple plaid boxer shorts bunched up around his furry ankles. My new phone. I'd freakin' left it home again.

With my bug-eyed boss standing over me, I stared at the photo with laser-like intensity until the image disintegrated. Totally disappeared. Right in front of us. As I rose and held out his cell, I felt the hairs on the back of my neck stand up. "I...I don't know what you're talking about, Mr. Fernández. *I* don't see anything here."

Slack-jawed, he snatched his phone and began swiping. "It was here two seconds ago...that...that stupid looking dog on a commode!"

Evidently, Jack Russell had not succeeded in "hypoopnotizing" Bill Fernández.

"Don't think," continued my boss, practically choking himself as he tried to loosen his too-tight navy necktie, "that you're gonna get out of this simply by deleting it."

My legs gave way as I flopped back into my seat. *"I didn't delete anything."*

"Ms. Rodriguez, I may delete your upcoming week of vacation," declared Fernández. An expression of smug righteousness on his gaunt face, he turned on his heels and strode out of the room, his shiny black oxfords squeaking.

I slumped over the audio board and exhaled.

Last night, the door opening all by itself...the glass of ice water dumping itself on Gneeecey's head...and now, *this*.

Shivering, I reached for the bottle of antacid that I kept stashed underneath the chipped beige counter and took a generous swig.

✳ ✳ ✳

FERNÁNDEZ WAS RIGHT. Here it was, nearly noon, and I had only just put the final touches on the Grunts commercial.

That's because Fernández wouldn't, or couldn't, stop meddling.

Every five seconds, it seemed, he would burst through the studio door, veins popping out all over his balding, egg-shaped pate. "Ay, *bendito*," he'd mutter, "estás volviendome loco!"

"Yeah," I'd reply under my breath each time, "and you're driving *me* nuts, too!"

It always turned out that I had produced whatever spots and programming he'd accused me of not finishing, like the promos for a new bilingual Hollywood gossip show. The teasers had been running six times an hour for the last week. Just keeping his scrawny butt in his too tidy office and bothering to check the program logs, or actually listening to the always booming radio on his desk, could've prevented ol' Bill from tearing out hair he couldn't spare.

Each time I'd proven my innocence, he'd slink out of the room, head hung low.

Until this morning's fiasco.

Time to set my houseguest straight. Sighing, I reached across the controls for the clunky old studio phone. Decided to punch in my mobile number first. My stomach acids churned as I listened to it ring. And ring and ring. I groaned. Gneeecey could play with my cell, but he couldn't freakin' answer it.

I muttered some choice words and slammed the receiver down. Then, in my peripheral vision, I detected motion.

No one else was in the room. Heart pounding through my ribcage, I lurched out of my chair just in time to see a luminous pair of lime-green eyeballs float past my face, through the doorway and out into the dimly lit corridor. I heard muffled laughter echo out in the hallway.

Shivering and perspiring at the same time, I collapsed back into my seat, frozen, for maybe five minutes. Finally, I grabbed the phone, and with trembling fingers, rang my home landline. Again and again. And again.

After about my tenth attempt, Gneeecey finally picked up. "*Whaaat?*"

"Diroctor," I whispered, "the bad guys, they *did* follow you here! Your Markman buddies...I...I just saw a pair of *eyeballs* float by!"

"Not now, ya lousy Ig! I'm watchin' *Oprah*!" Click.

-4-

AIN'T NO PLACE LIKE HOME

THE MUSTANG'S BRAKES howled bloody murder as I stopped short, giving myself whiplash. I peered up the steep driveway at the plateless, grayish wreck of a vehicle that littered my parking spot.

I lunged out of my car and tore up the pavement toward the side entrance, nearly spraining my ankle in a greasy pothole. Freakin' door was wide open.

"Gneeecey! Gneeecey!" I hollered, rushing inside, gulping for air. "Where *are* you?"

Ear-shattering silence.

Until Gneeecey's shrill voice suddenly screeched from the next room, "Yeah? Really? It's springtime on this side of the planet!"

I flew down the staircase. "Someone there with you? Gneeecey! Answer me!"

"That's *Diroctor* Gneeecey," the canine-humanoid informed me, traipsing into view. "An' ya jus' interrupticated my stinkin' phone conversation. I was *talkin'* to someone."

"Who? Where?"

"Dunno. Think I dialed a wrong number. Used your landline, so don't worry, you'll find all that out when ya get the bill. We talked for a coupla hours—till *you* started yellin'."

"You just wait a minute here."

"The guy, whoever he was, lives in a priddy interesticatin' country, upside-down somewhere on the other side of your Earth. Couldn't even understand half of what he was sayin'."

Blood pressure rising, I scooped the day's mail, mostly bills of course, off the wooden ledge. He'd pay for that long-distance call, one way or another.

"Okay, Diroctor, now, whose, uh, car is out there on the driveway…parked in my space? And why did you hang up on me? The bad guys! I saw one of 'em! They *did* follow you here! And how dare you use my cell phone to take that stupid selfie of yourself on the freakin' toilet and then send it to my boss and his bosses? You sure didn't hypnotize *them*!"

"So many questions, Ig! Slow down, for Bogelthorpe's stinkin' sake, slow down!"

While my bleary eyes settled on him, the rest of the kitchen came into focus. Looked like a sewer had exploded. Dark liquid, splattered all over, dripped down the glossy white cabinet doors onto the matching countertops. The double sink was piled on both sides with every pot and pan I owned. Brown blobs, what looked like coffee grounds, gooped-up funnels, measuring cups, and utensils littered the floor, along with a half-dozen torn-up boxes of my store brand flavored gelatin. Even the cat-with-the-wagging-tail clock seemed to frown down upon the mess.

I gasped. "What the…"

"Hadda make me some decent coffee, Ig. Didn't wanna get a stinkin' headache."

"You…you did *what*?"

"Made summa that orange an' lemon-flavored blobby stuff an' mixed it wit' your coffee. Y'know, that coffee in that big yellow can that'cha had hidden high up in that caboobinet behind lotsa other stuff, but I found anyway? Hadda borrow Rico's ladder to stinkin' get to it. Oh, an' by the way, he fixed your stooopid shower."

I threw my mail at the table. "*Not my good coffee!*"

"Yup, Ig. Used it all. Only thing missin' was rindom extract. Couldn't find none in this lousy dimension of yours. Coffee didn't even come out bitter. Ain't like my Merk Perk back home." He held up my handle-less WUGG mug, filled to the brim with jigglin' joe. "But'cha know, Ig, it didn't come out thaaat bad, if I say so myself. Ya can still eat it wit' a knife an' fork."

Mumbling words that most likely weren't real, I plopped into the only clean chair in the room.

"An' ya know what else, Ig? I made dinner, too. Mastered, whaddayacallit, ethnic cookin', in jus' *one* afternoon!"

"Huh?"

"Cooked us rice an' beans! Well, I cooked the beans. All I hadda do was dump five of them Goya cans into a coupla them there big pots. Won't hafta cook for *days!*" He pointed to the stove.

I bolted upright. "*Five of my Goya cans?*"

"Yeah, they all smelt sooo good goin' into them pots! Was kinda surprised I even liked any stuff of yours. That's why I kept openin' all them cans an' pourin' 'em in."

Slumping, I cradled my achy head in my hands.

"Didn't cook the rice, though. Woulda got *soft* if I prepooparated it like they said on the package."

"Yeah," I growled. "I forgot. Where you're from, everyone eats screws and bolts."

"An' tire gauges, too, Ig. An' ya know what else?"

"No. What else?"

Gneeecey grinned. "I fixed your TV so it gets *Oprah* reruns. All day long. In fac' it don't get nuthin' *else*! An' I meant to ask ya, how come whenever there's a commercial for products for dirty an' smelly stuff, they always show *dogs* in 'em?"

I leaped to my feet. I loved *Oprah*, could watch her all day long, every day. That is, if I had time to do anything but work. But it was the principle. "You messed with my TV?"

"Oh, an' Ig, 'fore I forget, some weird guy named Carlos called."

My eyes widened. "*What*?"

"Asked if he could pick ya up at seven-thirty tonight, insteada seven. I tol' him ya hadda cancel. Ya had other more important plans an' ya didn't have no time for him tonight."

I took a step toward Gneeecey. "You *what*? How *dare* you?"

"He seemed kinda maaad an' asked me who I was but I didn't tell him 'cause I figured it wasn't none of his stinkin' business. An' I crossed your salsa dancin' lessons off of your calendar for tomorrow night..."

Fists clenched, I took another step toward him. "I'll say it again. How *dare* you?"

"Easy, Ig, easy! I need ya tonight, to take me to your dopey motor vehicles office to get plates an' junk for my new car. An' tomorrow night, ya gotta take me to..."

"*Your new car*?"

"Well, it's new to me. That beaudiful automobile sittin' out there on the driveway! Was lucky to get one in pastel black. Such a priddy color!"

My jaw dropped.

"An' after motor vehicles, ya gotta take me to that auto store up the street. Gotta ask 'em 'bout the fallin' apart exhaust system's probooblem wit' carbon trioxide."

"*You bought a car while I was at work?*"

"Yup, Ig. Gotta get around while I'm livin' here, which may be quite a while."

I felt lightheaded. "You…you…"

"Rico's friend's uncle-in-law's brother's cousin's dad had this lovely vehickookle for sale. Right nearby, in Hackookensack. Nice guy. He was so happy I bought it that he had it delivered here, right to our door."

"*Our* door?"

"Price was right, too, only a grand!"

My muscles tensed. "So, I imagine you paid for it with that thousand-dollar bill you, uh, retrieved from Yammicles' mouth, right?"

"Nah, Ig. Wanna save that one for myself. I saw in your desk ya had all these funny Visa checks wit' papers talkin' 'bout how smart it is to transfer balances an' save lotsa mon-ney an' get lotsa stuff ya want. Y'know."

"*What?*" I took another step toward Gneeecey, and he fell backward, into a chair.

"Ooow! My stinkin' bimbus! An' my tail—I mean, I forgot to pick up my *mail*—"

"You used *my* checks?"

"I was doin' ya a favor, Ig! Honest! On them checks it said how ya hadda use 'em up by a certain date or they wouldn't be no good no more, an' how they'd be real hapoopy if ya used 'em, an' I didn't want them real important financial people to get maaad at'cha, so I…"

I smashed my fist on the table, right into a quivering glob of coffee. Several chunks flew into his face. "You used *my* checks? You forged *my* signature?"

Blinking, Gneeecey bent down, picked a gooped-up spoon off the floor and began to lick it. "I practiced writin' your name a whole buncha times," he volunteered, between slurps. "Finally got it perfec'. Came out priddy good if I say so myself. Nobody won't know the difooference, Ig."

"Do you realize what you did?" I wiped the glop off my hand with a paper napkin and, on my way to the trash can, crumpled it, imagining that it was that piece of rusted junk out on the driveway. "You know, I can make a call right now and have you…"

He jumped up. "Arresticated? You'll do nuthin' of the stinkin' sort, Ig. Yoooou still owe meee! Bigtime!"

Teeth clenched, I pivoted.

He shrank back. "Heh, heh, now be a nice Ig. I'll pay ya back. One of these days. Can't tell ya which one, though."

Swearing that the top of my skull was about to blow off, I lifted him up into the air. "*I want this whole freakin' kitchen cleaned up. Right now!*"

"Okay, okay, Ig! Ya made your point. Put me down!"

I dropped him and stared, through narrowed eyes, at the mess surrounding us.

Suddenly, a searing flash of white light blinded me, and an invisible force smashed me up against the brick wall. Couldn't move a muscle. Felt like I'd been sucked inside a jet engine.

A deafening clatter ensued. The very fabric of time seemed to stretch.

After an eon, there was stillness.

When my eyes opened, the entire kitchen was sparkling clean, every single item back in place. And two dinner plates sat side-by-side on the pristine table, piled with mounds of steaming rice and beans, savory aroma beckoning.

Gneeecey gawked at me. "How in Bogelthorpe's name did ya do *thaaat?*"

-5-

SOMETHIN'S GONE TERRIBLY WRONG

"IG, I STINKIN' ASKED YA, how'd ya dooo that? Ya even cooked the rice!"

"I dunno." I staggered into the living room. "Now, you get that grimy fur tail of yours in here. You've got some real explaining to do."

"Wha'cha *mean*, Ig?" asked Gneeecey, scuttling along beside me. He looked almost childlike.

I collapsed into my office chair and stared straight ahead into the bedroom. My now empty marmalade jar, lid face-down, of course, and a gumped-up spoon, decorated my rumpled bedspread.

Gneeecey gawked at me from over the mountain of bills heaped on my desktop, only his bulgy peepers and the top of his fuzzy noggin visible. "Ya know, Ig, you've changed since ya lived in my mansion. I don't think I like ya no more."

"Oh, you mean you liked me before?"

After a pause, he replied, "Not really. But, now you're creepin' me out. An' looky!" Hopping like Perswayssick County's hyperactive kangaroo mascot, he raised his right foot high above my pile of papers. "Whatever ya did in the kitchen there, ya even busted my stinkin' sneaker!"

Sure enough, the front of his rubber sole had partly detached…and the sneaker *was* stinkin'.

"Y'know, Ig, it's actually priddy cool 'cause I could hide stuff in there. Now, getting' back to what we were jus' disgustin', you're totally creepin' me out."

"Diroctor, I've decided I'm not taking crap from you or anyone else anymore. Too bad if that scares you. Uh, what is that round red blob on my pillow that I can freakin' see from here?"

"A pluot."

"A *what*?"

"Guy on the corner said it's some kinda mutant plum—part apoopricot an' part somethin' else. Sorta reminded me of them sloggenberries we got back home on my planet, so I traded the busted radio in my new car for it."

I rose and headed for my trashed bedroom, tripping over Gneeecey's blasted civil defense helmet. "Thought I asked you to put that freakin' thing in the closet."

He wrinkled his snout. "Why don't yooou?"

Jaw clenched, I swiveled.

Gneeecey's eyes grew as big as two grapefruits. "Okay, Ig, okay! *I'll* stinkin' do it!"

I watched as he scooped up the gaudy piece of headgear, chartreuse propellers still spinning, and scurried into the bedroom.

As the closet door creaked open, an unearthly multicolored light permeated the place.

"*Fleaglossity!*" shrieked Gneeecey.

Knees quaking, I hobbled through the doorway and gazed into a vivid rainbow of light.

There stood Gneeecey's black-furred canine-humanoid pal Sooperflea, (real name Fleaglossity Floppinsplodge, and nicknamed "Flea"), frozen, encased in what appeared to be a translucent, multi-colored holographic test pattern. Only his mouth moved. "Somethin's gone terribly wrong…somethin's gone terribly wrong," repeated the red-caped superhero, in a spooky, deep voice.

"Holy stinkin' Saint Bogelthorpe!" yowled Gneeecey as he swung his hard hat into the closet and slammed the door shut. The eerie light oozed through the edges of the doorframe.

Gneeecey stuffed Yammicles into his T-shirt pocket and practically knocked me over as he sprinted into the kitchen.

I flew after him. "You come back here!"

"I am soooo outta here, Ig!"

"Good!" I hurled his purple rubber briefcase at him.

It bounced twice and unlatched itself. Two cobalt blue eyeballs floated out, accompanied by low-pitched, echoing peals of laughter.

"Yaaaaaaaaaaaaaaaaaah!" Gneeecey leaped up into my arms and screeched those dreaded words. *"Threeeee fordy-twooo bluuuuue!"*

After the purple fluorescent flash, everything went black.

-6-

UH, MAKE THAT CHAPTER "SICKS"

I BOLTED UPRIGHT, thrashing about in a sea of warm, waist-deep mush. "I can't freakin' see!" "Well, then ya can't believe," replied Gneeecey, matter-of-factly. "What?" I screamed.

"Y'know what you Earth humans always say, Ig. Seein' is believin'."

"You and that platitude-spouting snout of yours. Now, you've really done it."

"Done what, ya lousy Ig?"

Tears burned down my cheeks as I scooped up a handful of crud and hurled it in the direction of his voice. "You know we're never supposed to say those words when we're near anyone, much less touching someone else. You went and shouted 'em when we were physically attached."

"So?"

"So, remember the last time you did that? We ended up stranded in that weird intermediate dimension, filled with those ice crystals."

"Yeah, Ig, I do rememboober. Didn't know if up was down or down was up or if we'd live or die or ever get home again. An' it was kinda real freezin', too."

"*Yeah.*"

"Well, don't say it like that, so oogdimonious."

I slapped the sludge. "I'll say it any way I want. Now, I've got kind of a problem here. *I can't see. I'm blind!*"

He chuckled. "It's proboobably jus' tempooporary."

"You know, everything's been upside-down and screwed up ever since that hideous day I first met you. Then, when I finally escape back to my own dimension and start putting the shattered pieces of my freakin' life back together, guess who shows up?"

"Who?"

I exhaled. "*You.* You barge back into my world and mess everything up again, even worse than before."

"Well, Ig, y'know what they say," he replied in a righteous, singsong tone. "You can't unscramble the omelet."

"I'm gonna unscramble you!"

"Don't stinkin' forget, Ig, yoooou invaded my lousy dimension first."

"Yeah, right," I growled, a mixture of panic and anger coursing through me.

"See, even *you* agree."

As I lurched his way, my sight began to return. Slowly but surely…and unmistakably…the ugly Perswayssick River Bridge, and the miles of glistening brown, noxious mierk that coated the riverbanks, came into view. My heart plunged down into the pit of my stomach, splashing up bile along the way. With a groan, I pointed to the dull-finished, several-mile-long steel structure, a strange bridge that spanned the entire length of the river instead of simply crossing it. "Freakin'

Perswayssick County. I'm stuck in *your* dimension again. This time my life's *really* over." I punched the muck with all my might.

"Don't blame the mierk, Ig."

"You just don't get it, do you? My life is ruined! I'll lose my freakin' job, which, thanks to you, is in real jeopardy now, and…"

"Ain't that a TV show?"

I smashed the mierk again, with both fists. "And I'll lose my apartment. I'll never see my family again. Or my friends. Or Carlos. And there goes my trip to Paris."

"Ah, home, sweet stinkin' home. Looks like I'm back in time for F-Day." A self-satisfied grin spread across Gneeecey's gunk-splattered face. "An' I can still get them secret codes outta ya. In fac', it'll be much easier here on my own turf."

"And, you know, Diroctor, there goes my credit rating, too, right down the toilet! That thousand dollars you put on my Visa account for that…that piece of…"

"Thousan' bucks ain't nuthin', Ig."

My head was about to explode. "Whaddaya think I am? A freakin' millionaire?"

"A million ain't nuthin'. *I'm* a zillionaire."

My mouth opened wide, but only guttural grunts escaped.

Gneeecey reached into his T-shirt pocket, surfaced with my new cell phone and began fumbling with it. "Lemme call Altitude to come pick us up…hey, this lousy thing ain't workin'."

"Give me that!" I snatched my possession from his grubby mitts.

"I stinkin' forgot. Your stooopid, compooplicated phone won't do us no good here in my dimension anyways, ya Ig."

I glanced down. Sure enough, no towers. Sighing, I crammed the useless, multitasking thing into the back pocket of my blue jeans. "And once and for all, will you stop calling me 'Ig'?"

"Okay, Ig. Now looky here, my beaudiful new state-of-the-art smellphone here should do the trick. Got me a newer model after that disaster wit' my Binky the Clown phone fallin' into that dumpster fire." Smiling, he thrust an orange plastic kangaroo, the size of a deck of cards, in my scowling face. "Meet Mister Kangoogaroo, the latest, mos' advanced communications device from BlunderBuxxComm. Leaves youse Earth people's teckooknology in the dirt. As usual."

"You're *sittin'* in the dirt," I half-whispered. "As usual."

The canine-humanoid flipped up the grinning marsupial's head, unsnapped its pouch and began pressing some bright purple back-lit keys embedded in its belly. Several moments passed. I could hear rapid, high-pitched beeps as the number he called rang and rang. His smile became a scowl. "Why ain't that dope Altitude pickin' up? That lousy, no-good oversized mouse. Stinkin' sixteen years ol' an' thinks he knows more'n *I* do."

"Everyone knows more than you think you do," I mumbled.

His eyes darted my way. "*Whaaat?*"

I cleared my throat. "Uh, nothing."

Gneeecey slapped Mr. Kangoogaroo's noggin down. "Well, Ig, we're gonna hafta walk until we run into a bus or cab, or one runs into us."

"Hope one runs into you," I muttered, resisting a powerful urge to kick him.

"Don'cha worry, Ig. I know this place like I know the back of my hand. Oh, looky, what's *thaaat?*"

A slimy sky-blue question mark, its dot a giant purple-veined eye, stared up at us from Gneeecey's knuckles, then hopped down. Matching azure dragonfly wings attached to both sides, the tiny translucent thing skimmed the glop below as it half-flew toward more of its kind, a moving mountain of monochromatic stained-glass panels.

Gneeecey gawked, fascination and horror etched on his face. "Kinda disgustipatin'. Ain't never seen such a interesticatin' species before. So ugly, they're actually beaudiful."

"You're, uh, mierk looks a bit anemic," I observed, shuddering, trying not to think of the undulating mound of insects as I scooped a glob of gunk off the ground with a stick. "Hmmm... not as brown as usual, is it? Thought this noxious stuff was outlawed after that election of yours."

Gneeecey's eyes narrowed. "After we lost that stooopid election I tried to fix, where them dopey environmentalists got their stinkin' way, they started a cleanup of these here riverbanks. They call it redivlopment. I'll extra-never, *nebberd-kinnezzard* believe that mierk is poisonous. My fight ain't nearly ovoover."

I leaped to my feet. Must've been nuts, just sitting there in the toxic mess. "Well, Diroctor, you still have your, uh..."

"My stinkin' whaaat?"

"Your neurological speech impediment."

He glared my way. "I ain't got no speech impedipoodiment!"

"Diroctor, listen to yourself. *Ovoover. Proboobably. Impedipoodiment!* Remember what your neurologist Dr. Idnas said?"

"Stinkin' nope."

"C'mon. You do. She said that you and everyone else in your Perswayssick County were coming down sick because of your precious, poisonous mierk."

"She don't know nuthin'. An' you don't neitherwise."

"*My* speech problems disappeared as soon as I got away from you and all your goop."

✻ ✻ ✻

"I'M FREAKIN' LEAVING HERE as soon as I can. And when I do, I never want to see your face again," I shouted at Gneeecey's rounded back. "I don't even care if my dimension burn gets worse. At least I'll get away from you!" The sun fried me as I marched down the dirt road. The large patches of mierk that soiled my clothing dried instantly, flaking off and falling to the ground with each step I took. "I mean it. You and I are so done. *Over!*"

"Stinkin' whatever, ya lousy Ig," replied Gneeecey as he waddled ahead of me. His droopy tail trailed behind him, drawing a long, crooked line on the parched earth below.

I groaned. "Must be nine hundred freakin' degrees out here."

"That's not skientifically possibooble, Ig. Nine hundred degrees, we'd be pudoodles, not peopooples."

"I know your seasons come earlier than ours on Earth, but this is ridiculous."

"Proboobably globular warmin', Ig," he replied, looking over his shoulder. "Got that here in my lousy dimension, too."

"Well, Diroctor, I'd give my life for a bottle of water." I glanced skyward and came to a sudden halt. "*Holy crap! Two suns!*"

Shielding his eyes with both hands, Gneeecey gazed upward. "I only been gone one stinkin' day, an' now we got two suns?"

"I remember you mentioning that your Planet Eccchs has a binary star system…"

"Walk quicker, Ig. Gotta get back into town an' see what in Bogelthorpe's name's hapoopening. I left Flubbubb an' Stu in charge."

I shot the panting Gneeecey a sideways glance. "You left those two in charge?"

"Yeah."

"Seriously?" Flubbubb Finial was Gneeecey's childhood pal, or more accurately, childhood frenemy. A handsome but not overly bright golden-furred canine-humanoid, the freelance percussionist even worshipped the ground that Gneeecey sat on. But Gneeecey treated him with utter contempt. As for the good diroctor's annoying brown-nosing donkey-humanoid WGAS-TV intern Stuart Pitt…well, Stu couldn't cut it either. Not even with a pair of sharp scissors.

"There's a madness to my method, Ig. Even together, them two ain't got 'nuff brains to grab any of my power. But, I betcha that Bassett Hound jerk Jacob Qwertyuiop is gonna try. Well, ain't nobody takin' over my title of Grate Gizzygalumpaggis of this fine county or my Quality of Life Commissioner gig neitherwise. Jus' wait till I fix that stinkin' runoff election nex' month."

Some things never changed. "And what about poor Sooperflea?"

"Whuddabout Flea?"

I stopped in my tracks. "Your best friend, Sooperflea!"

"Whuddabout Fleaglossity?"

I blinked. "Your childhood buddy Flea is back in my dimension, trapped in that…that freaky solid test pattern, in my bedroom closet. Don't you even care?"

"Got more important junk to worry 'bout."

I shook my head, took a deep breath and resumed walking.

"Well, he stinkin' got my civil defense hat to protec' him," added Gneeecey, a trace of guilt evident in his tone. "Rememboober, I threw it at him right before we ran?"

That moment, a bright kelly green vehicle zoomed into our midst, creating a dust storm as it skidded to a stop.

"A Perswayssick City taxi!" Waving his dirty mitts in the air, Gneeecey rushed over to the rapidly opening driver's side window.

"*Your Grate Royal Hynesty!*" gushed the plump, red-maned zebra-humanoid cabbie. His horizontally striped mesh black-and-white T-shirt, decorated with Z's and B's, made him look like a living crossword puzzle. "What an abject honor to run into *you*! In *person*!"

Gneeecey ate it up. "Yupperooney, it's your lucky day for sure, my royal subject. You've come upon meee, The Grate One, your county's one an' only Grate Gizzygalumpaggis. Grate Gizzy, for short. Y'know, I pride my stinkin' self on savin' vowels an' consonants."

"I like your new title," replied the awestricken zebra.

Gneeecey's head tilted. "Ain't new."

"Oh. Sorry. Anyway, may I have the extreme honor an' intense pleasure of transportin' Your Grate Royal Hynesty an' his lovely companion home on this most suspicious occasion?"

"Yeah, but she ain't my companion. An' she certaintaneously ain't lovooverly. She's jus' my stinkin' assistant, the Ig."

"In your dreams," I muttered, seeing stars as I kicked a rock that turned out to be half-buried in the ground.

"Well, c'mon in," said the zebra, winding up his window. "Suns are settin'. Be dark soon."

Gneeecey shoved me. "Get in, ya Ig."

The skies were clouding over and the humidity seemed to be rising by the second. I placed my hands on my hips and stared at the good diroctor through narrowed lids. "Get in your freakin' self."

Suddenly, Gneeecey flew sideways, at supersonic speed, into the backseat, bashing his brains out on an inner door handle. He flashed me a look of pure hatred. "Ow! How dare ya push me, ya lousy Ig?"

"I…I didn't even touch you." I shrugged and slid in after him.

The zebra turned up the air conditioner full blast. The first frigid gust slapped my moist skin, giving me instant goosebumps.

"Ain't never seen *you* 'round these parts, Mister Zebra," said Gneeecey, rubbing his injured dome. "Ya new or somethin'?"

"Nah, Your Grate Royal Hynesty. Me an' my family have lived here for years, for as long as we've had two suns. Name's ZeeBee. Got a twin brother. He's a zombie."

Gneeecey's rapidly blinking eyes caught mine. "Uh, Mister ZeeBee, lemme tell ya where I live." An uncharacteristic quaver had hijacked his vocal cords.

The driver chuckled. "Oh, no, Your Grate Royal Hynesty. Everyone knows where *you* live. It's a hysterical landmark."

"Well then, why are ya turnin' here on Sicks Street?"

"It's more direct than Well Street or even Fifth or Fourth. It'll getcha home much quicker, Your Grate Royal Hynesty."

"Mus' be me, or mayboobee that lousy hit I jus' took on my dopey noodle. 'Causa *her*." Gneeecey glared my way. "I don't even rememboober any of these streets. Stinkin' whatever. Keep drivin'."

"Yes, Your Grate Royal Hynesty. An' you know, Sire, I gotta mention, you sound kinda different in person than you do on TV. Your voice is a little higher an' you got less of an accent."

Gneeecey and I exchanged puzzled glances. He started to gnaw on his wrist.

"No worries, Your Grate Royal Hynesty," said the zebra, eyeing us in his rearview mirror. "I'll have you home in no time."

Sneaking a look at my muddied ruby red slides, I began to plan my escape, only to drift off into a dream. Something about being lost in a dark, freezing forest, where all I could hear were shrill voices cackling up in the branches.

I WOKE WITH A START as our cab began the long, nearly vertical ascent up mountainous Bimbus Crack Drive, to Gneeecey's four-story stone mansion, a veritable castle, topped by four chimneys. My ears had popped like crazy on my first ride there, too, already months ago.

Darkness had fallen.

Gneeecey's lush, spotlighted plaid lawn finally came into view. The good diroctor bolted upright. "Hey! I didn't give nobody no permission to dye my lousy lawn *purpoople*—it was stinkin' *greeeeeeeeen* when I left!"

"Mus' be some kinda misunderstandin', Your Grate Royal Hynesty," offered ZeeBee. "I'm sure you'll sort it all out."

Gneeecey lunged out of the cab. "Whatever I stinkin' owe ya for the lousy ride, jus' put it on my account."

"Why, he don't owe me *nuthin'*," said ZeeBee, turning to me as I disembarked. "His Grate Royal Hynesty always takes care of us. Y'know, like he always says, he gives us the shirts off our backs!"

"Haaah?" Gneeecey glanced back over his shoulder for a moment, then tore toward his home's entranceway. "Junk is all difooferent!"

It sure was.

"Someone stinkin' moved my steps from under the livin' room window," he yowled. "Dopey perpoopetrator put 'em back under the *front door*! Won't fool burgooglars no more!"

His cheap green-and-white doormat that I remembered from my first unwitting visit, monogrammed "GIT," still languished in the mud below. But, the gilt italics above the doorframe that should have spelled out, "Residence of the Grate One," instead read "Residence of The Grate BigButtKizz."

Bug-eyed, Gneeecey raced up the stairs. I followed, hot on his heels.

He plunged his fist into his shirt pocket and surfaced with a handful of jingling keys. One by one, he attempted to insert each one into the golden lock, with no success. "What in Bogelthorpe's stinkin' name is goin' on?" he howled as he kicked and punched the polished, red-stained mahogany double doors over and over again. *"I'm locked outta my own lousy house!"*

The elegant portal squeaked open slowly.

We froze.

In the foyer stood a duplicate Gneeecey. "What is with all the ruckus?" he demanded, staring down at us.

-7-

WHEN GUINEA PIGS FLY

GNEEECEY BARRELED INTO the mansion's musty, dimly lit entrance hall. "Whooo in Bogelthorpe's lousy name are yooou?" Smoothing the lapel of his inky smoking jacket, the other Gneeecey frowned at his double. "I am Ebegneeezer Eeeceygnay. Whooo in Piggwinkle's wrinkled pink rump are yooou?" He spoke with a British accent and in a slightly lower-pitched voice than that of the good director.

Gneeecey's peepers bulged out of their sockets. "Wha'cha doin' in *my* stinkin' house?"

"*Your* house? I'll have you know, old chap, this is *my* house! Has been forever-and-a-half! For as long as we have possessed two suns! And this house did not reek until *yooou* darkened its doorstep!"

The two stood nose-to-nose, toe-to-toe, fists clenched.

Gneeecey scowled. "Oh yeah?"

"Bloody affirmative!" growled Ebegneeezer. His left eyeball glowed a luminous purple.

Gneeecey stumbled backward, nearly knocking me down the front steps. I was too freaked to protest.

Somehow, I recovered my footing and hopped up onto the blue-gray marble floor. Ebegneeezer unfurled his right mitt and wagged two forefingers in my face, the extra digit located just above the first one. I blinked. He possesed a total of eleven fingers, six on one hand and five on the other. "And yooou, my darling little Igglitt, what are you doing with this blooming imposter? Why have you brought him here, to blight our fair residence?"

"I…I…"

"Did he attempt to interrogate you regarding our election results? And what mishap has befallen your usually lovely hair?"

"I…I don't know what you're talking about," I all but whispered as I ran a hand through my damp, dirt-caked locks.

Ebegneeezer's pulsating gaze became purpler by the second, melting whatever was left of my brain.

"And what do we have here, my dear, wonderful, awesome boss?" inquired a young woman, floating into view. *Holy crap*! She was my exact double, even wore her hair the same way, except that it was coal black, rather than blond. Her burnt almond eyes expanded to the size of saucepans when she saw me.

My mouth opened wide enough to accommodate a seven-quart Dutch Oven.

The other me folded her arms and looked me up and down, regarding me with a mixture of pity and contempt. "Poor imitation. And yikes! We'll have to do somethin' about that 'do. Maybe shave it all off and start over again."

My legs began to buckle.

"NickNick, be a good little Igglitt and go get Jerko," Ebegneeezer ordered my lookalike, cheek muscles twitching visibly beneath his fur.

"At once!" As his anger intensified, so did the blaze of light emitted by his strobe-like left iris.

I gulped.

"Yes, dear, wonderful, awesome boss," replied NickNick, flashing long, sharp fingernails.

My Gneeecey grinned, watching her sprint out of sight on sneakers that were a color I'd never seen and could only describe as being black and white at the same time, but neither, with a touch of red that seemed blue.

"And yooou," Ebegneeezer warned, his extra forefinger poking the sunburnt tip of my nose, "shut that big aperture of yours before a commercial jet airliner mistakes it for a hangar and glides right in."

"That's what *I* always stinkin' tell her—she should shut her dopey mouth," volunteered Gneeecey, forcing a laugh as he attempted to score points.

It didn't work. The good director's lookalike shot him the dirtiest of looks. "Quiet! You two walk ahead of me. And please do not attempt anything foolish." Ebegneeezer tossed what appeared to be a crumpled soft drink can up into the air, caught it in his yapper and swallowed it whole. "Into the parlor, I said. Now, not the Piggwinkling day after tomorrow!"

Freaked, I studied the six-foot expanse of multicolored vapors that lay between us and the parlor. "What kind of floor is that?" I asked. "It's not solid—we'll fall right through!"

"Yee-haw!" yelped Gneeecey as he darted past me and did a belly flop into the vortex.

"What is wrong with you two blithering fools?" asked Ebegneeezer, striding effortlessly across the floorless floor.

"Check me out!" hollered Gneeecey, up to his neck, splashing about in the smoky sea of rainbows. "It's like swimmin' in nuthin' that's supposed to be somethin'! This is a real cool house! It's proboobably really mine! They jus' redeckookerated it while I was gone an'…"

"What is going on here?" interrupted a severe baritone voice, attached to a tall Golden Retriever-type canine-humanoid female, clad in a white lab coat. A stethoscope hung from her slender, aristocratic neck. She peered down her long snout at Gneeecey. "Are you another one of my husband's uninvited relatives? Here to mooch?" she asked, speaking with an American accent.

Gneeecey's jaw dropped. *"Goonafina Blopperdang? My Goonafina?"*

She turned up her wet black nose. "I don't know *you*—and I'm certainly not yours! My name is Groonwaldina! *Doctor* Groonwaldina Eeeceygnay! I demand to know what you are doing in my house, messing up my floors!"

"Goonafina!" cried Gneeecey, jumping up and down in the multicolored whirlpool of nothingness. "Of *course* ya know me! Me an' you were engaged to be married—back on Planet Ecccchs, rememboober? But'cha jilted me by interdimensional email when I got stranded in Perswayssick County! Ya busticated my heart! How could ya stinkin' dooo that? Y'know, I'm a *zillionaire* now!"

"Ebegneeezer!" hollered Groonwaldina as she elbowed her husband, "I demand to know what is going on here! What is this rude stranger doing in my house?"

He reached down, snatched Gneeecey up by the neck of his T-shirt and flung him into an oversized translucent chair that reflected the ghostly floor's unearthly hues. "How dare you speak to my wife with such familiarity!"

"But me an' her…her an' me…"

"You and her *nothing*! I am positively going get to the bottom of all of this." Ebegneeezer turned to me. "Now, I *said*, walk across that floor!"

Just the sight of the swirling kaleidoscope made me dizzy, but I'd show him. Jaw clenched, I took my first step out into the void, then another. And another. Finally, I threw myself toward the glint of a highly polished parquet floor and crash-landed on my knees. Saw stars as I slid forward, relieved nonetheless to feel something tangible beneath me.

"Atta girl!" exclaimed a gruff voice. Swiveling, I came face to face with an all too familiar waxy-complexioned male crammed into a gray silk double-breasted suit a couple sizes too small. *Vicious blond big-nosed Mark.* One of Perswayssick County's most notorious mierk-covered floating eyeball gangsters. All named Mark, except for their leader Bob, they slathered and stretched the noxious muck over their invisible bodies to create skins for themselves. The Markmen, as I called them, had tried their best to kill Gneeecey and me back in Perswayssick County, not too long ago.

My heart nearly stopped.

Ebegneeezer slapped the guy on the back. "Hello, old boy."

"Heya, Boss," replied the burly man, leering at me.

"So, the dumb broad walked across the stupid floor," said NickNick, glowering as she grabbed Jerko's beefy arm. "What's so bleepin' great about that? We do it every day!"

My face hardened. So did hers.

"Heh, heh, *M-M-Mark*," stuttered Gneeecey. "W-w-what're y-y-yoooou doin' here? Ain't got your *mon-ney*, if that's what you're still after!"

"Name ain't Mark, pal. Ya mus' be thinkin' of two other people."

Groonwaldina's white canine teeth glistened. "Speaking of two other people, I demand to know, and right now, who are these strange visitors? And what are they doing here, in my home?"

Winking at me, Jerko cast aside NickNick's hand, reached into his tight jacket and produced a brown pistol. Its barrel flashed with multicolored lights. "That's jus' what we're gonna find out, right Boss?"

"Affirmative," replied Ebegneeezer, his purple peeper illuminating the dark room.

* * *

"BUT I STINKIN' NEED THE BAT'ROOM," insisted Gneeecey, dancing a lopsided jig on the gleaming oaken floor. "*Reeeal baaad!*"

Ebegneeezer cracked his fur knuckles. "Jerko, accompany this imposter to the loo."

"Aw, Boss, do I gotta?"

"Yes, you absolutely must. And you are not to leave him alone, not for a split second."

Groaning, the greasy gangster jammed his high-tech revolver into Gneeecey's spine. "So, walk awready."

As the two marched off into darkness, Ebegneeezer, NickNick, and Groonwaldina stood blocking me, their hateful glares broken only when after a loud bang, Gneeecey's bloodcurdling shriek pierced the air.

Sights fixed on the gloomy corridor, I pushed past Ebegneeezer. NickNick leaped between the two of us and dug her razor-like red nails into my forearm. Skin broken, blood dripping from the wound, I shoved her and ran. As I scrambled toward the bathroom, what appeared to be a black-and-white checkered guinea pig flew over my head, chased by two preteen female Golden Retriever-type canine-humanoids.

"Mister Gobblesnotts," they yelled in unison, "come back!"

"Lousy flyin' rat bombed my skull!" declared Gneeecey, waving his fists in the air as he ran toward us. Jerko lumbered behind, convulsed with laughter, firearm down at his side. The creep had to stop every few feet, to catch his breath.

Ebegneeezer gawked up at the ceiling. "The children's pet guinea pig keeps escaping."

"Hah, hah, Mister Gobblesnotts musta gobbled one too many," said Jerko. "He's droppin' bricks again." Still chuckling, he jammed his weapon back into his strained waistband and leaned up against the slate gray living room wall.

"Must be the new feed," said Ebegneeezer. "Less costly, but apparently lacking adequate fiber."

"I needed a good laugh," said Jerko. "At someone else's expense."

"Ain't funny," grumbled Gneeecey. "Shoulda been wearin' my lousy civil defense hat." His head whipped around in my direction. "*Yoooou* made me put it in the closet. *Flea's* stinkin' wearin' it now."

Chills ran through me, thinking of Sooperflea's plight back home. And now Gneeecey and I found ourselves in an unearthly predicament. We couldn't help Flea, and he couldn't help us, even if his ESP superpowers were working. That moment, I swore I could hear the superhero's voice murmuring, "Somethin's gone terribly wrong …somethin's gone terribly wrong." Maybe I was going loopy. I folded my arms and sighed.

Just then, NickNick sashayed into our midst. "I say we get ridda that horrid animal. Keeps flyin' into my room and stealin' stuff. Even took my car the other day!"

Gneeecey and I exchanged glazed glances.

"Dropped it, too, on the marble floor," she added. "When I took it out on the driveway and hit the Zx enlarger switch, I saw he'd even cracked my windshield! I vote we get ridda Mister Gobblesnotts."

"No! No! We love Mister Gobblesnotts!" yowled the girls, the larger one springing up into the air to recapture their pet. When she landed, the entire room seemed to shake.

"No, NickNick, we shall keep him," stated Ebegneeezer, his purple orb illuminating her stony face. "The children absolutely adore the filthy little furball."

"Yes, dear, wonderful, awesome boss," replied my double, her tight voice barely audible.

She seemed oblivious to the daggers shooting her way as I dabbed at my bleeding arm with a tissue.

"Yay, Daddy!" shouted the children, jumping up and down, the bigger one causing the room to quake again.

"These are my two lovely daughters," Ebegneeezer informed us. "Plumpa, my eldest, and my baby, VuVuzela." The two, attired in identical navy cotton jumpsuits, favored their mother.

"Yep, I'm the oldest," piped in Plumpa, shrill as a smoke detector, "even though I'm the smallest. But I do have this big bump of knowledge here on my head."

Sure enough, a golf ball-sized, fur-covered lump topped the scrawny girl's head.

"Daddy says I got extra brains 'cause I got extra smart parents," continued the young canine-humanoid. "Makes me special."

"My bump's hidden, but I got two capital V's in *my* name," honked VuVuzela, her voice a cross between a kazoo and a megaphone-amplified foghorn.

"Well, *my* name's got two *P's*," squawked Plumpa, as Gneeecey nodded in approval. A member of Perswayssick County's prestigious Alphabet Exchange, consonants, and vowels, for that matter, were coveted items.

"We're a consonant-rich family," added VuVuzela, cuddling Mister Gobblesnotts. "And my dad's real important!"

I smiled half-heartedly as my mind raced, preoccupied with escape plans.

Hopefully, Ebegneeezer, surrounded by his wife and children, would behave in a civilized manner. Maybe Gneeecey and I could sneak out of whichever guestroom we were assigned, while everyone else slept…just as long as we weren't locked in…then we'd have to exit through a window…hopefully a first-floor window. Whichever way we did it, once out, we'd have to find an isolated area immediately and risk our lives uttering those four words, and pray that we wouldn't wind up somewhere even worse. Just my freakin' luck to find myself in the company of two Gneeeceys…only this newer one seemed way smarter. Way more sophisticated. Way more sinister.

Grinning back at me, VuVuzela squeezed squeaky Mister Gobblesnotts under her arm and jammed a furry thumb up her runny left nostril.

"Y'know, I'm stinkin' *glaaad* I got dumped," muttered Gneeecey as he watched the child. He pinched my tender arm, causing it to bleed even more. I jerked away and pulled another crumpled tissue from my pocket. The deep injury inflicted by my lookalike was shaped like the letter N. A monogrammed wound.

Plumpa held up what resembled a colorful cardboard cereal box, her bright eyes flashing my way. "Daddy got us this book of Earth stories! *You* remind me of Earth!"

I barely managed another weak smile.

The youngster plunged a fist into the box, fished around and produced a living, three-dimensional scene, complete with red-clad girl, grinning wolf, and dark forest, all contained in the palm of her hand.

"Stinkin' *amazin'*," whispered Gneeecey.

"I'm tired of this story." She slammed the scene back into the carton, Little Red Riding Hood's screams echoing all the way down, "Help! Wolf's gonna get me!"

Groonwaldina shot her husband a stern glance. "Ebegneeezer, I wish you'd stop feeding the children all this nonsense."

"I enjoy making my daughters happy." He trained his supernatural orb on me. It seemed to click every few seconds. "And my children adore legends and memorabilia from *your* planet. We once owned a headless cat named Ichabod. Could not quite see where he was going, but he bloody sure felt where he'd been alright."

"*I* got me a cat that's half motorcycle," bragged Gneeecey, chest puffed out. "An' part Siameeesical."

"How…how," I stammered, ignoring Gneeecey, "do you know where I'm from?"

"I have my ways," replied Ebegneeezer, his intensified violet rays nearly blinding me.

"*My* cat's named Klunkzill," continued Gneeecey, not noticing that no one had noticed him. "Wit' two K's an' three L's. He drinks motor oil. High viscosity. Low maintenance. He'll live *forever*."

Suddenly, one of those tiny sky-blue question mark insects like those we'd seen on the riverbank alighted on VuVuzela's wrist. The slimy thing goggled at her, dragonfly wings fluttering.

"Honk! Honk!" she trumpeted, ground-pounding in clumsy circles and knocking over a tall brass lamp. "Get it off me! Get it off me!"

"It cannot hurt you, my little one." Ebegneeezer reached up, as she was taller, to flick the bug off her. "It is simply a melicoccus bijugatus parasite. Exclusively a threat to the *earthly* quenepa fruit. Harmless to you, my dear. How they got here, I can't imagine." Lavender light flickered my way.

"Noooooooooooooooooooooooo, Daddy! It's gonna get me!"

"*Reeeeal* glad I got dumped," mumbled Gneeecey, observing the child. He yanked Yammicles out of his lumpy T-shirt pocket and began to wipe his nose on the limp bear.

"Daddy! Daddy! He has my teddy!" bawled Plumpa, her tone so sharp that a nearby vase shattered.

Ebegneeezer's leather loafers crunched in the broken emerald green glass as he strode over to Gneeecey and whisked Yammicles out of his trembling hands. "How dare you steal from a child! *My* child!"

"But…but…Yammicles is *mine*!" protested Gneeecey, jumping up and down like a pogo stick. "I brung him here in my pocket! I can stinkin' *prove* it!"

"Look, Daddy!" Plumpa pulled a crinkled greenback out of Yammicles' torn muzzle. "An old thousand-dollar bill, just like they used to have on Earth! Can I keep it? *Pleeeease*?"

"How quaint," mused Ebegneeezer, smiling my way. "Probably from the United States of America."

"It's from *New Jersey*!" shouted Gneeecey, stamping his foot down hard. "An' it's *mine*!"

"Unlike our advanced civilization," continued Ebegneeezer, clearing his throat and chuckling, "they actually used currency."

"*Used?*" I half-whispered.

Ebegneeezer nodded. "Yes, my dear Plumpa, you may keep it. Deposit it in a safe place. Might actually be worth something someday."

"Oooooh, thank you, Daddy!"

Ebegneeezer crossed his arms. "And please do wash your hands after you put it away. These Earth artifacts are so very often, well, less than sanitary."

"Okay, Daddy! You're the best!"

"The bear an' the mon-ney's *mine*!" wailed Gneeecey.

"Whose image appears on that bill?" asked Ebegneeezer, smirking as he ignored his frantic, leaping lookalike. "Millard Fillmore—or Jackie Gleason?"

Tossing Yammicles to VuVuzela, Plumpa giggled. "No Daddy, we studied Earth presidents, back in Pre-K! It's Grover Cleveland!"

"Correct! That bump of yours holds so much extra knowledge! Now my darling girls, go upstairs and change into your pajamas, then I shall come read you a lovely story. Another Earth tale." With that, Plumpa and VuVuzela skipped out of the room, Gneeecey's precious possessions in tow.

"That currency or whatever ya called it is stinkin' *mine*!" screeched Gneeecey. "An' so's the bear!"

Ebegneeezer adjusted his ascot. "Jerko, escort these two fraudulent imposters up to, you know, the *little* room."

"The bad smellin' one up on the third floor?"

"Affirmative. *That* one. And be sure to triple-lock them in."

Gneeecey's eyebrows shot up. And my legs became limp noodles.

"Wit' pleasure, Boss."

Ebegneeezer snatched up the lamp that VuVuzela had toppled, and lifted it to his black lips. Gneeecey gaped as his lookalike wolfed it down whole, lightbulb and all, in a split second. "Wifey will not be overly pleased. This was an authentic replica of a copy of a duplicate of an antique from the Pre-Gneeezian era—maybe not all that rare, but extremely costly."

"C'mon, youse two." Chin jutting in my direction, Jerko yanked the pistol out of his waistband and dug it into Gneeecey's dimpled back. The good diroctor did his best to appear calm and collected, but his knees, knocking out sixteenth notes, gave him away.

Ebegneeezer belched sonorously, then proceeded to wipe his mouth on his silk sleeve with great vigor. NickNick sat nearby in an oversized multicolored armchair, sneering at me as she flipped through an equally oversized glossy fashion magazine.

Teeth grinding, my focus remained on my malicious double until she was barely visible through the white-hot haze that had begun to cloud my vision.

"Ow! Stop *looking* at me!" she screamed, wincing.

Jet engines reverberating inside my skull, I leaned up against the cold wall and squeezed my lids shut.

When the cacophony subsided, and I dared to open my eyes, I beheld four very lifelike statues. A modern-day Pompeii. Ebegneeezer stood motionless, forearm plastered to his muzzle. NickNick sat frozen, in the act of turning a page. An expressionless Jerko stared straight ahead, jamming his gun into a static Gneeecey's spine.

Ears still ringing, I raced over to Gneeecey and tugged on his stiff shoulder. "C'mon, Diroctor! *Now*! We can run right *past* 'em!"

Gneeecey remained rigid and unresponsive. Adrenaline surging, I slipped an index finger beneath his bulbous honker, relieved to detect a warm, moist hint of breath.

"C'mon, Diroctor!" I shouted again, turning to check that the others hadn't come back to life. "*Please!*" Tears welling up, I shook him hard.

Suddenly he jumped up in my face. "*Whaaat, ya Ig?*"

"Let's get outta here! Now! Before they wake up!" I scooped Gneeecey up and dashed toward the foyer, knowing that if I had made it across those vapors once, I could do so again.

"Jerko! Apprehend them! Immediately!" ordered Ebegneeezer.

"Nice try," rumbled the gangster as he tackled me from behind and took us down.

-8-

FREEZIN' HOT

I G! IG!"

Cringing, I rolled onto my side, on a mattress that must have been stuffed with gravel. Sharp gravel. "What? What now?"

"I can't seeeeeeee!" hollered Gneeecey.

"Well, we *are* here in the dark. Go back to sleep."

"I caaaaaan't! 'Cause I was never asleep yet!"

"Look, Diroctor, we're gonna need every ounce of strength we have, so we can try to make a break for it once those two suns rise."

"Ya don't understaaand, Ig! The dark in here is so bright it's hurtin' my ears!"

"I...I don't understand...how can..."

"An' I'm stinkin' noseblind!"

"Always suspected *that.*"

"Ya Ig, I can't seeeeee what I'm smellin'!"

"Do you usually?"

"Can't even stinkin' *taste* it!"

"What?" With a groan, I lowered myself onto the splintery wooden floor. It was more comfortable than the mattress.

"Ig, I smelt 'em talkin' out there, through the door," continued Gneeecey. "Yoooou musta been asleep. The guy who looks like Mark an' that other bad man wit' the purpoople eye an' too many fingers that's impersonatin' me an' talks real stupid an' funny like he's better than the rest of us, he said somethin' 'bout drivin' me an' you to someplace called Plumber's Crack, in the mornin', to get answers outta us."

I bolted upright. There was no light to turn on. "Don't you go loopy on me now, Diroctor."

"Ain't goin' loopy on ya, Ig. I jus'..."

"You just haven't taken your meds in a couple days." The realization smashed me over the head like an iron skillet.

"Didn't see wha'cha jus' said. Say it again, brighter."

"I *said*, you haven't taken your meds in a couple days. Especially your Bumpex and your Repulsid."

"Nah, Ig. Ain't that. I swear it ain't."

"It must be." I felt an icy draft from somewhere high above. Sitting cross-legged, I pulled what felt like a horsehair blanket, (and smelled like a horse), around my quaking shoulders.

"Well, Ig, it can't be the meds. Ain't seen no talkin' trees or walkin' chairs, have I?"

"I bet it's those vapors you were swimming in. You know, that floor between the foyer and the parlor that wasn't solid?"

"Ya mean, ya mean, I got *floor* poisonin'?"

"Something like that." I slid over and leaned back against the cold plasterboard wall. "Those fumes must've been toxic, and now you're..."

"I'm *whaaat*?"

I took a deep breath. A bitter odor, one I couldn't place, assaulted my sinuses. Reminded me of the stuff I used to clean my oven, back home.

Back home…back home…how I longed to be back in my own world…if even just to clean my undersized, half-working oven…something I always hated to do, when I could be working on one of my writing projects instead…oh, geez…would those floating eyeballs be roaming through my apartment when I got back? *If* I ever got back?

Suddenly, the entire building began to shake.

"Honk! Honk!" blared VuVuzela, racing about somewhere in the mansion, probably tormented by one of those slimy blue bugs.

After a minute or two, all grew quiet. Except for Gneeecey's voice. And a steady plunk, plunk, plunk, accompanied by a constant rhythmic clacking.

"Ig! Ig!"

I sighed. "Now what?"

"I'm freezin'. Freezin' *hot*!"

"What? How can you possibly be…"

"I'm sweatin' bullets! Can'cha hear 'em hittin' the floor? An' don'cha hear my lousy teeth ch-ch-chatterin'?"

-9-

A DESPOOPERATE SITUATION

MY EYES WATERED AS the rays of two rising suns poured through the high, vertical slit of a window. An open window. The polar blast that chilled me to the bone the night before had morphed into a balmy breeze.

Back still leaned up against the wall, coarse blanket scratching my neck and shoulders, I glanced around the colorless cubicle of a room, then down at my feet. There snored Gneeecey, curled up like a regular dog. "My mon-ney," he whimpered, between snorts. "My Yammicles...my Goonafina...my stinkin' house...ain't my *kids*, though..."

"Diroctor," I whispered, "wake up."

He jumped ten feet into the air. "*Whaaat was thaaat?*"

"Just me waking you. It's morning."

"Well, stop makin' all that blindin' racket! It's too stinkin' *bright!*"

I sighed, haunted by remnants of a dream. Could only recall Sooperflea's distressed expression and unintelligible mumblings.

Gneeecey shot up into my face, shattering my thoughts and very nearly my nose. "Ig! Ig!"

"What? What now?"

"*Looky!*" he wailed. "*Oh noooo! My haaands!*"

"What about them?"

"Dimension burn musta stinkin' done this!"

"Done what?"

"Looky, Ig—stinkin' *looky*! I got *ten* lousy fingers now instead of *eight*! I can't believe it!"

My eyes widened and my jaw dropped. Sure enough, Gneeecey's furry hands looked less cartoonish. He possessed ten digits.

"What am I gonna *dooo*? I got a real disaboobability now—I'm like youse *humans*! I stinkin' *hate* this place!"

Suddenly, two round aluminum platters came whooshing, one after another, through the crack beneath our door. Food sprayed in all directions as the trays scraped along the floor till they crashed into Gneeecey's red high top sneakers.

"Eat up, youse two," taunted Jerko, on the other side. "Ya never know, might be your last meal. Hah, hah, hah, hah..."

Gneeecey bent down, scooped up one of the dishes and slammed it into my solar plexus, spilling even more grub. "Here, ya Ig, *you* stinkin' eat it. Might be dangerousical."

I smiled. "Thank you."

He smiled back. "You're smellcome."

Shaking my head, I shoved the disk back into his mitts.

"Changed your mind, Ig? Ya scared or somethin'?"

"Diroctor, they're not gonna poison us yet. They want answers from us. Now, give it a try—you'll need your strength."

"Nah." He thrust it back into my hands. "You know I don't eat junk like that."

I took a sniff. "Apple slices and buttered toast. Smells good. Kind of like cinnamon bread. Here, Diroctor, at least try the toast. I don't dare. Probably isn't gluten-free."

"I said *nooooooo*!" Snout scrunched up as if he smelled rotten eggs frying on the Jersey Turnpike in July, he snatched the other tray up off the stained floorboards and dumped its contents onto mine. "Here Ig, now ya got *twice* as much."

I glanced down at my overfilled platter, then at him.

Cradling his empty dish, the good diroctor grinned sheepishly.

My sights remained riveted on him.

"Guess I *can* at least eat the dish," he conceded, raising it to his mouth. I could only gawk as he chomped it up and gulped it down, effortlessly. "Mmmm...real nice tinny aftertaste. I feel stronger awready."

"Uh, good." I set my plate down and flopped onto the mattress. "Ouch."

"Now listen up good, Ig. Me an' you, we gotta plan how we're gonna get back my mon-ney, my Yammicles, an' my Goonafina. Not the kids though. They ain't mine. Y'know, that baaad man who's impersonatin' me an' takin' all my stuff, he's..."

"You know, Diroctor, she's not *your* Goonafina, her name is Groonwaldina, and this isn't really *your* house."

He stomped his foot down. Hard. "Ow! Wha'cha mean?"

"I think we must've landed in some parallel universe."

"That's the stooopidest thing I ever heard!"

I threw my covers to the floor. "No! Listen! Now, in case you hadn't noticed, there are, just my freakin' luck, two of you. And two of me!"

"Yeah, I did notice, an' y'know, that other me's Ig is a whole lot nicer than my Ig."

"I am not your Ig."

He let out a loud, metallic-scented belch. "Well, I certaincerely wish you were more like her."

"Keep on wishin'." Speaking of wishing, I wished for coffee. Stomach rumbling, I reached over and lifted a thinly cut apple slice to my lips, then dropped it onto my lap, startled when from out of nowhere, Mister Gobblesnotts swooped down beside me.

"Lousy flyin' rat came in through that window up there!" shouted Gneeecey, shaking a fist at the animal. "Still ain't forgotted what he done las' night, defooficatin' on my dopey noodle! Get outta here, yooou!"

"Weeep, weeep, weeep," squeaked the guinea pig, paying Gneeecey no mind. The critter hopped onto my right knee and stared up at me with huge, shiny black peepers.

"Hi there," I said softly, stroking his checkered fur. "Want breakfast? You like apples? Here."

With four-fingered hands that featured opposing thumbs, he accepted my offering and began to nibble away. As the creature's leathery dragon-like wings rose from his hairless pink shoulders, I noticed an N-shaped scar. It matched the bloody wound on my arm.

"Yeah, ya Ig...feed the lousy little perpoopetrator," muttered Gneeecey. "Maybe he'll bomb your dopey noggin, too."

"Shut up." I handed Mister Gobblesnotts a tiny chunk of toast.

Gneeecey strode over to me. "*Whaaat?*"

"You heard me," I replied, glaring at him through narrowed lids. "Shut up."

That moment, Gneeecey zoomed backward and landed flat on his back on his rock-filled bed. "Ow! Why'd ya stinkin' do *thaaat?*"

"Do what?"

He sat up slowly. "C'mon, Ig, don't play dumb wit' me. Ya been havin' all these weird powers ever since I returnt to your world. Ya almost got us kilt last night."

"I…I…"

"Ya froze everyone, but not for long enough. Ya even froze meee! Then ya let all them bad people unfreeze too fast, before we could even stinkin' get away!"

I plucked another apple slice off the platter and gazed into space.

Gneeecey sprang up and clapped his hands in my face, causing Mister Gobblesnotts to flutter across the room. "Rememboober?"

My apartment door, opening itself…the glass of ice water, pouring itself on Gneeecey's head…that ridiculous selfie of Gneeecey atop my toilet, just disappearing from my boss's cellphone screen…my disaster of a kitchen, cleaning itself…the meal, cooking itself…Gneeecey, flying sideways into Mister ZeeBee's cab…me, walking across Ebegneeezer's gaseous foyer floor…last night, the folks in the living room all freezing into statues…and now, this…I couldn't deny it. I possessed some strange powers. Didn't know why. Or how to control them.

Shaking my head, I watched a mysterious, almost cartoon-like grin spread over Mister Gobblesnotts' fuzzy mug as he flew back over to me and snatched the piece of fruit from my fingers.

"Ya *hear* me, ya lousy Ig?"

"Uh-huh."

He scrunched up his muzzle. "Y'know, this is a despooperate situation. I mean, *I'm* the stinkin' Grate One. I'm a lousy genius, for Bogelthorpe's sake, got a certificate statin' so. An' even *I* don't know how I'm gonna get outta this disadvantical predikookament."

I sat up straight. "What about me?"

"*Whuddabout* you?"

"Well, in case you hadn't noticed, you're not alone in this mess. *I'm* here in it, too, right alongside you."

He bunched up his T-shirt and blew his honking nose into it. "Well, ya Ig, got any more dopey advice for us then? Here, I'll save ya the stinkin' trouble. Why don'cha jus' freeze the whole dumb universe? Jus' don't use your powers on meee no more."

I dug my nails into my palms. "Don't act like this isn't partly your fault."

"Wha'cha mean, *my* stinkin' fault? If it wasn't for yooou, me an' Yammicles, an' my thousan'-dollar bill, would all be back home safe watchin' TV, in my beaudiful, scenic, wonderfooful Perswayssick County!"

I folded my arms. "You're kidding, right?"

"Why stinkin' would I, ya Ig?"

"And would you freakin' stop calling me that?"

"Okay, Ig, sure. An' here, I jus' got me a great idea. Why don'cha go get yourself one of them flashy superhero outfits, y'know, wit' a red cape, like Flea's. Then ya can fly all over the place—real, real far away, I hope—an' get someone *else* kilt."

My eyes bored into his, my response startling even me. "I don't need a costume. I've got my *mind*."

He shuddered visibly.

"You know, we *will* get out of this, one way or another," I continued, overcome by a sudden, albeit fleeting, sense of peace. "I've always believed that a one-legged person can win a butt-kicking contest if they just jump high enough and kick fast enough."

"Well, Ig, I got one butt an' two legs, so your lousy advice ain't gonna do meee no good."

"You know, Diroctor, we're never gonna get out of this whole mess if we fight with each other. We'll have to pull together, you and me. To survive."

He nodded. "Hate to stinkin' agree wit'cha, Ig, but you're proboobably right."

We both jumped when the humongous top door lock clicked and turned. "Okay, youse two," boomed Jerko. "It's *time*."

Squealing, Mister Gobblesnotts leaped off my knee and flew out of the window, in a single bound.

-10-

PRIDDY IN PINK (AND EVERY OTHER COLOR IN THIS CHAPTER)

SIX-FOOT-TALL TEAL ALLIGATOR stood framed in the double doorway, decked out in a loud yellow plaid zoot suit, accented by an enormous matching neon bow tie. A boring tan suitcase sat by his scaly, boat-sized bare feet.

"There *is* no room to let!" growled Groonwaldina as she slammed both doors in the grinning gator's face.

"The blue alligator again?" inquired Ebegneeezer.

"Mus' be a spy," offered Jerko, gun aimed at Gneeecey and me. "He's been comin' 'round ever since you won the last election."

"Well," snapped Ebegneeezer, "why do I employ you? Dispose of him."

The gangster lowered his weapon and gazed down at the scuffed brown oxfords that didn't really go with his needing-to-be-cleaned gray suit. "Yeah, Boss, okay. I been tryin', but it ain't that easy. There's like a *few* of him an'…"

"And be mindful of the pistol, Jerko," warned Ebegneeezer. "Do not drop it again and shoot another hole in your trousers, or worse, shoot one of *us* in *our* trousers."

"I'm sick and tired of interruptions when I'm trying to watch my figuring skating," interrupted Groonwaldina as she stomped over the vaporous foyer floor, back into the dark, television-lit parlor. "These are the *Intergalactic* Figuring Skating Championships! Can only see them once in a green znurgglesnort, that is, if I don't have to go into the office or teach."

"Yes, my dearest Groonwaldina," replied Ebegneeezer. "I know how you absolutely detest interruptions even when you are interrupting me." His attention returned to his bodyguard. "I did not forget *you*," he said as his left eye shot a purple beam into Jerko's scarlet face. "Mind you, my children are in this house."

After several seconds, the blinking gangster shook his head and raised his revolver. "Okay, youse two," he ordered Gneeecey and me. "Siddown. Over there." He marched us over to a small transparent couch adjacent to a jumbo version where Groonwaldina sat, flanked by her daughters. The three sported strange twinkling spectacles, each pair fit with long, thin twin telescopes.

"Ain't never smelt glasses like thaaat," remarked Gneeecey.

I sighed. "You're still smelling what you see, Diroctor?"

"Yep, Ig, an' them glasses smell humongous, to use one of your weird igspressions."

Plumpa, lounging in red pajamas, glanced our way. "We spectators need these special optiscopes to see the invisible math problems the skaters are solving on ice."

VuVuzela, wearing a chartreuse nightgown, nodded. "That poor guy just got deductions 'cause he landed on the wrong edge of his blade when he skated the plus sign. Wrong answer, too."

"I can skate all my multiplication tables," bragged Plumpa, scratching the bump on her furry golden head. "And square roots, too!"

"Back in my ol' collogical days at the university, I did a mean triple klutz," volunteered Gneeecey. "Once I was competin' in one of them tourniquets an' I jumped so high, I got all tangled up in the ropes! An' a power line! Brung down the whole tent!"

The girls giggled.

"Now," continued Gneeecey, a smile spreading across his face as he addressed Plumpa, "why don'cha be a real nice little girl an' gimme back my thousan'-dollar bill and my teddy bear. You're real bright. Ya know they ain't really yours."

"*Daaaaddy!*"

Ebegneeezer leaped into his flinching lookalike's face. "How *dare* you? You leave my children alone!"

"Yeah!" bellowed Jerko, jutting his heavy jaw in Gneeecey's direction. "You're gonna find *yourself* on ice. You'll be one of them problems them skaters are tryin' to solve if ya don't chill out!"

"You know," I ventured, adrenaline surging, "that thousand-dollar bill and the teddy bear *do* belong to Diroctor Gneeecey here. I can attest to that."

"We're gonna attest to *you*," announced NickNick, waltzing into the room.

Jerko winked at me. "Hah, hah, hah. Wait till *she* gets through wit'cha!"

"You'll need to change out of that, uh, *outfit* you have the misfortune of owning," continued my double. She scowled at Jerko, then looking me up and down, tossed a jumble of garishly colored rags at my feet. "My favorite designer, Hari Cari. Last year's styles. Was gonna dump 'em, but givin' 'em to *you* saves me that inconvenient trip to the dumpster."

"That's my gal," said Jerko, still eyeing me. "Always helpin' poorer folks that ain't got, y'know, what *she's* gettin' rid of."

"An' the Ig sure is poor," piped in Gneeecey. "I should know—she works for *me!*"

"Not anymore," I growled. Nose wrinkled, I glanced down at the pile of puke-pink and lime-green castoffs on the floor. If I stared too long, the fabric would seem to move. I could hear Plumpa and VuVuzela cracking up.

"She got possibilities," said Jerko, his murky ocher peepers rolling my way. "Definite possibilities. She'll look priddy in pink."

"She'll never have what *I* have. And don't you ever forget that," warned NickNick, her sharp tone slicing through the air like a precision-thrown dagger.

It hit its intended target. Jerko winced.

NickNick's eyes flashed in my direction as she lunged forward and grabbed her man by his silk-covered sausage of an arm. He appeared to blush. "Your name," she began, "is Nicki. Mine is NickNick. Means I'm twice as good—at *least*."

"You're twice as *something*," I replied, just barely able to see her through the white haze clouding my vision.

She flinched. "Ouch! Stop *looking* at me!"

"Yoooou," said Ebegneeezer, as he motioned toward the small mountain of so-called clothes at my feet, "go change into these more sensible garments."

"Garbage is more like it." Face scrunched up like I smelled rotzels covered with spoiled cross-eyed cheese, (a real delicacy where Gneeecey came from), I kicked the multicolored mess. The girls snickered loudly, despite Groonwaldina's vain attempts to silence them, but not for my sake. She couldn't hear her skating competition results.

"Must I continually repeat myself? I ordered you to change!" boomed Ebegneeezer, both index fingers of his right hand waving in my face. "We absolutely must get going."

"But…"

"Blimey! I cannot take you outside wearing what you've got on!" he shouted. "You will draw unwanted attention!"

"Oh, like I won't, wearing this psychedelic crap?"

"Where ya stinkin' takin' us?" demanded Gneeecey, his voice extra squeaky.

"We informed you last night," replied Ebegneeezer, pulling on an expensive-looking khaki trench coat. "Plumber's Crack."

"See," Gneeecey whispered to me, "I smelt it right!"

"Yep, Plumber's Crack," repeated Jerko. "That's where we're takin' youse two."

"Where in stinkin' Bogelthorpe's name is *thaaat*?"

Ebegneeezer's left eyeball cast a lavender glow that illuminated the entire living room. "That is for us to know, and you to find out."

-11-

LIVES IN JEOPOOPARDY

UNDER DIFFERENT CIRCUMSTANCES, I would've been convulsed with laughter, cheek muscles cramping. The contraption that covered Gneeecey's dome, a rusty, upside-down bowling trophy, complete with periscope and mesh muzzle, resembled what might've been a sewer specialist's helmet back in the days of knights and armor, on some planet inhabited by medieval canine-humanoids.

"Shut'cha dumb trap an' waaalk," snarled Jerko. He dug his revolver deep into Gneeecey's pudgy back, creating a second dimple. Motivated, more or less, we trudged down the steep driveway that circled Ebegneeezer's sprawling acres of purple plaid lawn.

"I can't stinkin' *seeee* wit' this lousy thing youse peopoople put on my noggin," protested Gneeecey. "Youse want me to flop into your 'spensive green-an'-a-half bushes an' busticate 'em?"

"Ya *got* eyeholes." Jerko loosened his blinking battery-powered spiderweb-patterned necktie and unbuttoned his tight collar as he shuffled behind the slow-moving Gneeecey. *"Use* 'em!"

The good diroctor appeared to be a full foot taller than usual. He stumbled down the blacktop, smacking his ridiculous headpiece. "Why in Bogelthorpe's name do I gotta wear this stinkin' garbage can?"

"It simply will not do for me to be seen publicly with a lookalike," snapped Ebegneeezer, jogging backward. Attired in athletic wear, he sported a red muscle shirt, matching high tops that looked more expensive than Gneeecey's, and silky navy gym shorts. "A funny-looking lookalike at that."

Gneeecey growled.

And I came to a halt. "Oh, like nobody's gonna notice him wearing *that*? Or me, dressed in this idiotic Halloween crap?"

"Shaddup an' keep walkin'," ordered Jerko. The rays of the two suns reflected off shiny surfaces, blinding me.

Garbed in NickNick's poke-your-eye-out puke-pink and louder-than-loud lime-green hand-me-down rags, I felt like a two-ton cloud of cotton candy as I traipsed alongside Gneeecey. I could probably be seen from freakin' outer space. Which I had always loved…until lately. How I longed to be back on my own planet, in my own dimension…even if it meant slaving away sixty hours a week for Bill Fernández and eating peanut butter sandwiches in my freezing shoebox of a basement apartment. And what I would give, just to hear my mom's voice again…she had to be worried sick. How I prayed she that wouldn't go to my apartment to check on me and meet up with those floating eyeballs. Acid poured into my stomach, nearly causing me to double over in pain.

Gneeecey raised a grimy digit skyward. "Sure hope it don't participate. Ain't got no umbrellar, an' this here stooopid hat's proboobably gonna stinkin' rust even more if it rains."

"No *precipitation* in the forecast," replied Ebegneeeezer, voice laced with sarcasm as he put emphasis on the word Gneeecey had mispronounced. "Not for several yagwogs."

"Y'know, I'm stinkin' sick of your snarkasm!" exclaimed Gneeecey. "*An'* dumb accent."

"Oh really?" responded his lookalike.

"Yeah! Yeah an' a half!" Fists balled up, Gneeecey lurched in Ebegneeeezer's direction, his tall headgear causing him to veer into a shrub. I scurried over to steady the good diroctor.

"Thanks, Ig," mumbled Gneeecey, brushing himself off.

"Watch it, no sudden moves, or *I'll* make some ya won't like," threatened Jerko.

"I don't care if ya look like me or not, 'cause *I* proboobably looked like me first," said Gneeecey, ignoring Jerko. "Now, how dare ya corrugate my lousy English?"

English, I mused, as we slogged along. They all spoke English. Here, and back in Gneeecey's Perswayssick County, too. And on his Planet Eccchs. Apparently, all throughout the universe…just like in the movies. Never really thought about it much before. My brain hurt. A lot.

"Your lousy English *is* lousy," replied Ebegneeeezer, his purple left eyeball intensifying as it flashed Gneeecey's way. "*And,*" he continued, addressing me, "whatever language you expect to hear is what you are going to hear, wherever you *go* in this multiverse. That is just the way it is. And always will be."

Now, Ebegneeeezer was reading my mind? Despite the two suns burning my neck through my thick fluff-covered collar, I began to shiver.

"Okay, stop, youse two!" thundered Jerko. "Right here."

We froze in our tracks.

"Here's the car." Jerko pointed to a flat silver circle about three inches in diameter that sat sparkling on the blacktop.

Ebegneeezer bent down, and with his extra index finger pressed a red button embedded in the center of the gleaming disk. He leaped backward, as in a split-second the saucer expanded to the size of a compact, round vehicle. It resembled a UFO on wheels.

I gasped.

Gneeecey's lookalike smiled. "Consider yourselves fortunate. This is the most cutting-edge development in transportation available today. On this planet, only *I* and one other in my entourage possess these truly remarkable experimental pocket-car models. My little Igglett *loves* hers."

Jerko chortled. "Yup, an' so does Mister Gobblesnotts." Gun still aimed at Gneeecey, the creep reached with his free hand for a slim indentation barely visible on the side of the vehicle. A click later, an entire segment swung upward.

"Ain't nuthin'," declared Gneeecey. "Back home in Perswayssick County, *I* gots me a thirty-two-door limo. Slithers 'round corners like a snake an' the trunk's big 'nuff to carry my spare Porsche. Y'know, for 'mergencies."

Ebegneeezer's snout crinkled. "Who *gives* a heap of bleep?"

"An' back on Planet Eccchs," continued Gneeecey, "when I was a kid, a very smart one, I had a tricycle wit' three square tires. Ya shoulda seen how good that thing took corners. Didn't hafta wear no stooopid hat neitherwise!"

Ebegneeezer yawned.

"An'," added Gneeecey, glancing my way, "back in regoogoolar New Jersey, y'know, in *her* dimension, I bought me a bran' new used vehickookle. 1982. A very priddy pastel black. Ain't got one of them glossy, high maintenance finishes. An' I'm the *ninth* owner!"

I shuddered. My Visa card payment, (extra humongous this month no doubt), would be due soon. But here I was, stranded again. Hello, nightmare. Goodbye, almost repaired credit rating. Probably wouldn't even have a job to go back to. *If* I ever got back.

"Shaaaddup!" Jerko shoved Gneeecey's helmeted head down. "Backseat, youse two. In!"

"Caaan't! Dopey noodle ain't gonna fit! Lousy hat's too tall!"

"Jus' bend down your dumb neck," replied the gangster, who had real nerve calling anyone else dumb. Laughing, he shoved Gneeecey into the car.

"He can't ride the whole way like that," I protested.

"We don't need *your* alien input." The creep grabbed me by my shoulder.

I smacked off his beefy hand. "Keep your filthy mitts off me."

"Yeah?"

"Yeah!" I replied, smoldering on the inside. "I may look like her, but I'm *not* your stupid girlfriend."

"Hah, hah, ya could be! You're jus' as hot!"

I stared him down until that white haze clouded my vision. *You want hot, huh?*

He dared to touch my arm again, then flew backward, howling. "She burnt me! Little witch! She *burnt* me!"

I had done it again. Made something happen. Without consciously trying. "Touch me again," I snarled, "and you'll find out what it's like to *really* burn!"

"We shall see who is going to burn," declared Ebegneeezer, his supernatural eye fixed on me, as Jerko staggered in lopsided circles, moaning.

Standing tall, I stared right back at Ebegneeezer. "How'd you like someone to treat one of your daughters like that? *Think* about it."

Ebegneeezer winced. "What in Piggwinkle's wrinkled pink rump is wrong with you?" he shouted at his bodyguard. "Get in the car. *Now!*"

Glowering, Jerko obliged.

"Tryin' to get us kilt again?" Gneeecey whispered through his mesh muzzle-piece, as I slid beside him onto the rounded, well-cushioned bench seat. It was upholstered in some sort of translucent reddish fabric, a cross between velour and sharkskin. "Ya keep puttin' our lives in jeopoopardy!"

"I...I..."

"Yeah, Ig, stinkin' whatever," said Gneeecey, neck bent, ridiculous topper pinning him against the ceiling. "Nothin' won't matter no more anyways, when we're dead. Okay now, where's my seatbelt?"

"Ain't none," answered Jerko, still squeezing himself behind the car's sleek dashboard.

"Well, I don't wanna get seriously kilt or worse if this vehickookle crashes!"

"It is totally impossible for this vehicle to collide with anything," chimed in Ebegneeezer, sitting up front in the passenger seat beside Jerko. "Invisible bumpers have built-in state-of-the-art sensors that activate a protectionary guhnoozian force field. It has been tested at 4,000 GPG."

"GPG? What in Bogelthorpe's name is that?" asked Gneeecey.

"Galumphs per gneeeze."

"Well, back home, I got me a cow wit' a *clock* in her stomach," bragged Gneeecey, straining to be heard. "She's a alarm. Real advanced teckooknology. Installed her infrared sensors myself. No intruder will ever make it past her!"

"By the way," volunteered Ebegneeezer, poker-faced as he glanced over his shoulder, apparently unimpressed with his double's claims of electronic expertise, "I advise you not even to entertain any thoughts of escape. We have you both locked in from up here, utilizing special uncrackable codes."

"Ow!" cried Gneeecey, as our vehicle hit a bump. "*I ain't stinkin' uncrackable!*"

"You know," I appealed to Ebegneeezer, "I seriously doubt that anyone can see through these tinted windows. Please let the good diroctor remove that...that uh, *thing* from his head, at least until we get to where we're going."

"Nope," replied Jerko. "No way."

Ebegneeezer cleared his throat. "That is a somewhat reasonable request."

"But, Boss," protested Jerko, whipping his greasy head around, "we don't want no one to see..."

"Just keep your bloody eyes on the road, Jerko. Drive."

"Thank you." I slid the monstrosity off a grateful Gneeecey's perspired noggin.

Rather than reversing to back down the remainder of the driveway, Jerko yanked back on a long black lever. Instantly, the whole passenger compartment revolved on its base three times to face us in a forward position.

As the vehicle rolled down the long, winding stretch of pavement, Jerko pulled on another smaller shifter, and we felt a sudden sensation of being in a rising elevator. Seemed like we were gliding above the ground.

"We *are*," said Ebegneeezer, glancing my way, an all-knowing glint flickering in his peepers.

It was one thing when Sooperflea read my mind. He was our friend. But not this guy. Chills ran through me.

"Where's stinkin' Fleaglossity when we stinkin' need him?" asked Gneeecey, as if he had read my mind too. Maybe freakin' telepathy was a communicable disease.

"Flea's back home, trapped in my bedroom closet," I answered, still creeped out by Ebegneeezer, who sat, neck craned, grinning at me.

-12-

FRUMBLESNOXX

W E FLOATED DOWN Whaddayacallit Way. On both sides of the road, vivid orange leaves sprouted from thin, lumpy poles that resembled tree trunks, save for their chrome surfaces, polka-dotted with what appeared to be electrical outlets and USB ports.

Ebegneeezer sighed. "Ah, springtime, simply lovely, is it not?"

Jerko stifled a yawn. "Yeah, Boss. Extremely loverly."

"Yeah, *real* stinkin' lovooverly," piped in a drowsy Gneeecey. "Always did like springs. Fun to play wit', 'specially when they go boing, boing, boing all over the place."

Gneeecey's lookalike yanked a cell phone from his pocket. "I shall set the ogglometer for eighty-nine point one grognoogs. So much easier with this new app. Works a lot more quickly and effectively than those pesky manual settings on the dash."

"Yeah, Boss. Ones on the dash might as well be analog. Hah, hah, hah, hah. What's his face…Clay…Clive…Cleve…whatever…never got those bugs ironed out."

"You must mean *Clyde*, old chap," Ebegneeezer corrected him. "And true, he absolutely failed to do so."

My heart skipped a beat at the mention of the name Cleve. Didn't have the slightest idea why. Felt my face flush. I detected Gneeecey staring my way.

"Even so, this is still the most advanced form of transportation that exists today," continued Ebegneeezer, as both right-hand index fingers tickled the red symbols blinking on the screen of his ultra-slim device.

"*I* gots me a devicicle like that," offered Gneeecey, his high, nerdish voice echoing through the passenger compartment. "A devicicle as cool as a icicle. Newest smellular phone from BlunderBuxxComm. Makes my coffee an' does my taxes. Also waters my plaaants an' wipes my nose."

"Probably wipes your behind as well," muttered Ebegneeezer.

"*Might* wipe my bimbus. Does *yours*?"

"No, mine does not wipe yours," replied Gneeecey's lookalike.

"Hah, hah, hah, hah," chortled Jerko. "Good one, Boss."

The good diroctor cleared his throat. Loudly. "*Whaaaat* did ya stinkin' say?"

Ebegneeezer pulled a black cloth sleep mask over his peepers and tilted his seat back. "I *said*, by the time we awaken, we shall have arrived at our destination."

"Yeah, Boss," agreed Jerko. "An' I can use a little snooze, too. Was up half the night, plannin' for today. Drivin' is always the best time to sleep."

A wide-eyed Gneeecey glanced my way. I sat up straight. "You're going to *sleep*? While you *drive*?"

"No worries, youse two. We'll be there before we wake up." Jerko donned a pair of dark shades, clicked a lever and reclined all the way back, practically landing in my lap.

Grossed out, practically smelling him, I shrank as far back into my seat as I possibly could.

Gneeecey cracked his fur-covered knuckles. "Where we goin' while youse two stinkin' go to sleep an' get us kilt?"

Jerko adjusted his sunglasses. "Awready tol' youse. Plumber's Crack."

"Wheels automatically retract when we reach the Palabrian Sea," added Ebegneeezer. "Then we shall descend forty-nine grognoogs immediately before we hit dry land."

Gneeecey grimaced. "Hope we don't stinkin' hit it too hard."

The bodyguard yawned again. "Them two'll really enjoy the trip. Better than an amusement park."

Flames shot through my solar plexus. "What's going on here? You're *really* gonna sleep while you're *driving*?"

"We're all gonna *die!*" shrieked Gneeecey.

"Frumblesnoxx!" snapped Ebegneeezer. "Have you blithering alien fools never heard of cruising on automatic pilot?"

Gneeecey scratched his dome. "Guess so. Usually I jus' sleep audimatically when my delivery boy Altitude drives. He's a mouse."

I shuddered, flooded suddenly by memories of Gneeecey's sullen protégé. The oversized young rodent had recently replaced the six-foot tall albino mallard Culvert who, until he quit to work a less stressful job on a farm closing turkeys' mouths when it rained, had driven the good diroctor's fully articulated zillion-doored white limo.

The firestorm in my stomach spread to nearby organs as Ebegneeezer and Jerko snored loudly upfront. I swatted Gneeecey's knee. "This is even worse than the time you drove with that freakin' box of animal crackers over your head, and we crashed into that milk tanker."

"Don't keep bringin' *thaaat* up, ya Ig. Yeah, so I busticated the dopey truck, but I got insurance plus I got to dunk my *aminal* crackers in all the spilt milk all over the street, so it didn't go to waste. An' besides, my lousy Porsche didn't have no damage or nuthin' an' I *did* stinkin' manage to get away from the police an'…"

"Those *animal* crackers of yours almost got us killed."

"Are you stinkin corrugatin' my lousy English too, ya Ig?"

A tremendous thud, one that bashed my soggy brain against the inside of my skull, interrupted our conversation.

"Wheels retracting," announced a smooth robotic female voice.

I gazed through the window, focusing my watery eyes on a green sign that jutted out of brilliant foliage. "Palabrian Sea," read its bold white type.

In less than a heartbeat, the car plunged into an ocean teeming with translucent whale-sized mylar balloons. Falling forward, I dug my fingernails into the soft sides of the seat in front of me, desperate not to have physical contact with the snoozing Jerko.

"*Holy crap!*" I shouted.

In an instant, those very words appeared, in elegant red script, scrolled across an elephantine inflatable. It slammed into us, and we veered sideways.

"Ig!" howled Gneeecey. That moment, a giant blimp with royal blue block capitals labeling it "IG" floated our way and bounced into our windshield, knocking us back several hundred feet.

"*Quiet,*" I whispered, eyeballs bugging out.

"*Whaaaaat?*" screamed Gneeecey, as a humongous green-marked silver blob collided with us, too fast to even be read. We clung to each other as our vehicle whirled violently. After the longest minute ever, the spinning stopped.

"Y'know, Ig," Gneeecey said, spitting in my ear, "this reminds me, once I bought some mylar sympoopathy balloons, kinda like these, but much smaller wit' black writin', an' I was gonna bring 'em to Cleve's funeral, but I thought you'd get real maaad if I brung 'em an'…whassamatter, Ig? Why are ya lookin' at me all weird like thaaat? I *didn't* stinkin' bring 'em, so ya didn't hafta get real maaad…hey, are ya maaad *now?*"

"Quiet!" Shaken in more ways than one, I glanced up front, where miraculously, Ebegneeezer and Jerko continued to doze, undisturbed. "Let's just try and stay calm."

Instantly, a couple of sausage-shaped aqua-lettered balloons smacked into our automobile, buffeting us back and forth. "Quiet" and "Calm," painted on their sides, they rocked us to sleep.

-13-

JUS' ASK OL' MOTHER GOOSE…OR OL' MOTHER HUBBARD

GNEEECEY TUGGED ON MY SLEEVE, ripping off a fistful of puke-pink feathers. "Stinkin' place is creepy." "And freakin' hot," I added, perspiration building on my upper lip. NickNick's polyester ostrich-themed costume clung to my damp torso like a plastic bag.

"Well, ya lousy Ig," continued Gneeecey, "jus' imagine how I feel wearin' this piece of garbage they stuck back on my dopey noggin. Weather ain't too good in here neitherwise. Can't hardly respoopirate!"

Flanked by Ebegneeezer and Jerko, we inhaled exhaust fumes as we lumbered through the amber-illuminated basement of what appeared to be a multilevel parking lot. A place, I imagined, where anything could happen to you, and no one would ever know. Or care.

Trekking up and down rows and rows of what looked to be conventional Earth vehicles, I could've been back in my own dimension. But I wasn't.

"Got the car, Boss?" inquired Jerko.

"Affirmative. Right here," replied Ebegneeezer, displaying it in his palm. "Rather stifling down here today, is it not?"

Huffing and puffing, Jerko tore off his suit jacket and tossed it over his shoulder. "Yeah, Boss. I'm sweatin' like a pig. Shoulda dressed like you."

"Solar panels must be absorbing both suns today. Too much efficiency. They are designed merely to utilize one. We must have Steve check that out."

"Yeah, Boss. Squiggleman needs to get on that right away."

"*Steve Squiggleman?*" blurted Gneeecey.

Ebegneeezer stopped in his tracks. "*Yooou are acquainted with Squiggleman?*"

"Yeah. Good friend of mine. Sold me three high-tech terlits. Even let me try one out in his store. Mechanical Bull 2000. Thing threw me, right in his lousy front window, durin' rush hour. Everyone on Murgatroyd Avenue saw. Made him an' his store look reeeal bad."

"See?" snapped Ebegneeezer, addressing Jerko. "It is nonsense like this. How in Piggwinkle's wrinkled pink rump does *he* know our Squigzy?"

"No worries, Boss. Where we're takin' him, we'll flush out all the answers we need, plus a few more. Hah, hah, hah, hah…"

"That is entirely right." Ebegneeezer shoved his lookalike. "Move along!"

"Hey!" Gneeecey careened sideways and nearly poked my eye out with the periscope that topped his headgear. Ducking, I managed to steady him and preserve my sight.

Seemed we were being led in circles. After we slogged our way past a line of cars identical to one we had already walked past several minutes before—featuring the same dirty orange knit cap drowning in the same oily puddle next to the same red convertible sporting the same personalized plates that read "JOKE ON U"—Gneeecey came to a sudden halt. He stomped his sneakered foot down hard and pointed a grungy finger at Ebegneeezer. "Why're ya tryin' to confuse us by makin' us walk 'round in circles through this lousy parkin' lot that ya don't really need to be in 'cause ya awready parked your dumb car in your hand so we won't know where we stinkin' are?"

"Smart chap," replied Ebegneeezer. "Just answered your own question."

"Yeah, too smart for his own good," said Jerko, brandishing his pistol. "Now, who told youse to stop walkin'? Move it!"

Before we could comply, Gneeecey and I found ourselves staring up at a couple of humongous three-eyed translucent eggs, one orange, and the other purple. Mouthless, their blubbery bodies shook like shivering gelatin. Their deep peals of laughter reverberated through the cavernous garage and vibrated through the floor and my racing heart, like an over-amplified bass guitar.

"*Holy Saint Bogelthorpe!*" squawked Gneeecey.

As I stood slack-jawed, an ether-like arm flowed forth from the orange entity's essence, growing until it reached Gneeecey. A hand sprouted forth. "Greetings," said the egg, in an ultra-deep voice, through a suddenly appearing fast-spinning hoop of a mouth. "I am Dumpty."

"Buh…buh…buh," stammered Gneeecey, his fur visibly standing on end. He grabbed me by my torn sleeve.

"And I," said the purple one, extending a lengthening arm, "am Humpty." Their lime-colored grapefruit-sized peepers spun in all directions when they spoke.

"We are the Blobbert brothers. Bwaaa, haaa, haaa, haaa!" they bellowed in unison, as Gneeecey's knees, and mine, too, knocked out some strange rhythms.

"Won't you two be sociable and say hello to Dumpty and Humpty?" asked Ebegneeezer, tapping his foot impatiently.

"Ya *mus'* mean Humpty an' Dumpty," replied Gneeecey, suddenly emboldened, flinging my arm away.

"No," asserted his lookalike. "I mean Dumpty and Humpty. I should know. They are employed by *me.*"

"In all the fine classical litooterature I researched back in my ol' collogical days," countered Gneeecey, puffing out his chest and pulling in his gut, "Humpty always came before Dumpty...it ain't natural no other way. Or correct, neitherwise."

"Oh *really?*"

"Yeah. Jus' ask Ol' Mother Goose. Or Ol' Mother Hubbard. Both reknowndicated scholarly scholars."

Ebegneeezer's purple eye blazed. "Seriously?"

"Yeah an' a *half.* I'll say hello to 'em, in the right order. But I ain't gonna shake their, uh, slimy haaands."

"You two, just follow Dumpty and Humpty," ordered Ebegneeezer. "We shall see you both up in the office after we remedy a certain matter."

"Yeah. An' don't try nuthin' stupid," added Jerko, glancing back over his shoulder as he and his boss disappeared into the shadows.

Hmmm...a chance to escape. I grinned. Gneeecey's tall helmet tilted sideways, as if he had read my mind.

"Come with us!" roared the two rotundities as their arms dissolved back into their bodies. They threw themselves to the ground, bounced several times, then began to roll forward on their sides. Slime oozed from them, orange from Dumpty and purple from Humpty, leaving a glazed residue on the cement floor.

Gneeecey and I ventured forward. When, miraculously, we didn't slip in the multicolored mess, we exchanged glances, pivoted and made a break for it, in the opposite direction.

A split second later, we found ourselves somersaulting in midair and landing hard on the concrete. Gneeecey's helmet clanked sonorously and cracked in half.

"*Owwwwwww!*" he cried, crumpled in a heap. Wind knocked out of me, I sat frozen in the vivid gunk, seeing stars and planets. My right leg had to be broken.

"Bwaaa, haaa, haaa, haaa!" thundered Dumpty and Humpty, as with impressive agility, they sprang upright. "You didn't have a chance. It's *forward* slime," added Dumpty. "Won't *let* you go backward!"

Able to draw breath once more, I rose, relieved that my throbbing limb could bear weight.

Gneeecey leaped to his feet. "I'm *maaaaaaad* now!" he spluttered like a wet hen. "Real, real stinkin' *maaaaaaad!*"

Fury welling up inside me, I stared at the two rogue eggs as their chortling echoed through the garage. My narrowed eyes remained riveted on them until they stopped jiggling and stood motionless.

I grabbed Gneeecey's hand. "C'mon! This is our last chance!"

"Okay, Ig!"

We took a running leap sideways, to avoid the colorful slick.

"Yee-haw!" shouted Gneeecey. "I am *sooooo* outta here!"

Abruptly, I found out what it was like to be a shelled, hard-boiled egg, sucked into a narrow-necked glass bottle during a school science experiment. I found myself trapped, barely able to move or breathe. Nothing but orangeness all around me. "*Holy crap!*" I yelled. I'd been swallowed by Dumpty.

I could just about hear Gneeecey's cries. "*Now* ya done it, ya lousy Ig! I'm stinkin' stuck inside Humpty! In his disgustipatin' *stomach!*"

"Bwaaa, haaa, haaa, haaa!" boomed the blobs as they rolled forward, with us inside them. My brain shook like jelly. Make that marmalade.

-14-

RED IS THE NEW BLUE

EBGNEEEZER LEANED OVER ME, a pint-sized scarlet parrot perched on his extra index finger. The canine-humanoid's breath stank of cigar smoke and garlic, and a metallic odor I couldn't quite place. "I said," he repeated, exasperation creeping into his tone, "you now must keep him on your shoulder."

"*What?*" I blinked as I sat cross-legged on the cold gray tiles, spitting tangerine flavored bits of orange gelatin into a tissue. My right leg no longer hurt. Couldn't even freakin' feel it.

"Are you dense?" he screamed. "I *said*, you now must keep Ol' Blue on your shoulder if you are going to go around looking like *that*."

"Go around looking like *what?* I don't understand."

He rolled his bulgy eyes. "Of all people, *you*, from your backward planet, should understand. You are only wearing one earring!"

My face flushed as both hands shot up to my ears. One of the gold hoops my dad had given me on my sixteenth birthday was indeed missing.

"Finders keepers!" boomed Dumpty, his three rotating eyeballs gleaming triumphantly.

An arm, complete with blobby hand, sprouted out of his left side, that is, if a round glob could have a side. It began rubbing his blubbery belly. "Yum! *Eighteen karats!* Much tastier than eighteen carrots, cooked or raw!"

"Don't *ever* give it back!" yelled Humpty, bouncing up and down on a nearby desktop.

My heart sank as Dumpty belched.

Meanwhile, Ebegneeezer had placed Ol' Blue on my shoulder. The bird, light as a feather, squawked, "Heya alien, heya alien! Where ya from?"

I leaned against the rough-textured wall and studied the stained drop ceiling. What would Ebegneeezer want to know next? How many holes were up there?

"Ig's from Earth," volunteered the ever helpful Gneeecey.

"Earth!" screeched Ol' Blue, hurting my ears. "Funny place! Funny place!"

"An' *she's* funny, too," added Gneeecey.

"Yeah?" asked the heavy-footed Jerko, bumbling into our midst. "How funny?"

"Well, not *that* stinkin' funny." Gneeecey sat across from me, spewing purple chunks of Humpty onto the floor. "After all, she invaded my dimension. An' that ain't funny."

A sharp-clawed bird dancing on my collarbone, I was too preoccupied to protest.

"Well, you both invaded *my* universe," declared Ebegneeezer. "And we are going to determine exactly why. Immediately."

"Yup, Boss." Jerko lowered himself onto a flimsy folding metal chair. It creaked as his weight shifted.

"We'll tell you *everything* you want to know," I replied, shocked as the words slid out of my mouth.

"Yeah an' a half," agreed Gneeecey. "An' how come ya call that there bird 'Ol' Blue' when he's really red?"

"Ol' Blue *is* blue," stated Ebegneeezer, matter-of-factly.

Gneeecey nodded. "Now that ya mention it, he *is*."

"Yes," I concurred, stunned once more. I mean, I could see that the freakin' bird was red.

"Matches my tank top as well," said Ebegneeezer. "It is also blue."

"Yes," Gneeecey and I replied in unison, gazing at his ruby shirt.

"Obedient, ain't they?" Jerko popped a stick of gum into his yapper and ran his fingers through his greasy yellow hair, chuckling between chomps.

"Absolutely, without a doubt," replied Ebegneeezer. The overhead fluorescent lighting made his fur appear almost ghostly. "We must work quickly now…before the substance wears off."

"Not to worry," boomed Dumpty, slapping his stomach. "Plenty more where that came from."

Ebegneeezer shook his head. "You and Humpty must conserve it for ZomSect3. Even though you chaps are superb multitaskers, you can only produce but so much. Our prison population is increasing by the day." He shot us a glance. "And it is about to increase by two more."

Gneeecey and I exchanged glazed glances. "*Prison* popoopulation?"

I shrugged.

"Stinkin' whatever," he mumbled.

"Yup." I spat a couple more pieces of Dumpty into my tissue. "Whatever. I guess… you know."

Ebegneeezer crossed his arms and smiled. "Now, this is *precisely* what we appreciate. Cooperation."

-15-

A LITTLE SPOON MAKES THE FOOD BIGGER

EBEGNEEEZER WHISKED THE CHAIR from underneath Jerko, pitched it up into the air and swallowed it whole. Burping, he turned to an awestricken Gneeecey who sat perched atop a tall stool. His high tops didn't reach the floor. "I once ate a motorcycle," volunteered the good diroctor. "Studyin' for finals, when I was a student at the good ol' University of Hardenoxx, back on my beaudiful Planet Eccchs. Ate a whole red motorcycle. Was proboobably blue, come to think of it. Had a little help from some friends, of coursickles."

Ebegneeezer tapped his foot impatiently, unimpressed.

"Sophoophomoronic stress, ya know?" continued Gneeecey.

"I *demand* an answer!" shouted Ebegneeezer, waving his hands in the air. "Tell me why there is pie in the sky."

"Yeah," piped in Jerko, still flat on his back, his two murky eyes-that-you-could-almost-smell spinning in opposite directions. "Tell us why's there pie up there in that dumb sky."

Ebegneeezer belched again, even louder.

"There's burpin' laws, y'know," warned Gneeecey, left brow raised as he addressed his lookalike. "All *over* the stinkin' universe."

"True," said Ebegneeezer. "But I only enforce laws when they apply to someone else."

"Me too," agreed Gneeecey. "Grate minds do stinkin' think alike. An' that would be spelt G-R-A-T-E…"

"Stop changing the subject! I demand an immediate answer!"

I squirmed in the squeaky wooden chair they had ordered me to sit in, wondering where this ridiculous line of questioning could possibly lead.

"That ain't a *askin'* question," Gneeecey corrected his lookalike. "You're sayin' ya want a *answer*, but you ain't *askin'* for one, so it ain't a *question*. People can only answer *askin'* questions."

"Alright then, I'm *asking* you. Why is there pie in the sky?"

Gneeecey scratched his noggin. "So the lousy chicken could cross the road?"

"No. And now you are asking *me*. Try again, you blithering twit."

Gneeecey stared ahead at the scuffed buff wall. "Perhaphoops to keep the sky from fallin'. Or, uh…um…proboobably to keep the sky's pants up. An' this time I didn't *ask*. I *answered*."

"Wrong!" shouted Ebegneeezer, ripping a chrome pencil sharpener off the wall and biting a chunk out of it. "Totally, absolutely positively wrong!"

"Not right, either," added Jerko.

"Y'know," growled Gneeecey, "like I *said*, ain't no stinkin' answer to your lousy question 'cause it ain't really a question. It's one of them fake, false, make-believe questions designed to trick me. An' you absitively posilutely *know* it."

Ebegneeezer spat out a mouthful of metal. The pieces clanked to the floor. Several bolts rolled underneath the desk. "It would not be a question if there were no answer."

"Yeah? Well, there ain't no answer, so it ain't really a question!" snapped Gneeecey, as he began to gnaw on his left wrist, just above his watchband.

Ebegneeezer's eyes widened. "My, you *are* hostile."

Gneeecey smiled. "Thanks! Where I come from, that's a severe compoopliment!"

"Here, as well."

I shook my head. The two Gneeeceys were alike in more ways than either would ever want to admit.

Ebegneeezer scowled at Gneeecey, then pointed his two right index fingers my way. "I expect some plausible answers from you two interloping and, I must add, utterly exasperating aliens."

"Well," I began, "then give us some freakin' plausible questions!"

Both Gneeeceys shot me daggers.

I smacked my Gneeecey's leg. "Whose side are you *on*?"

"Whichever side the chicken crossed to. Y'know, to avoid gettin' hit by the lousy apple pie up there in the sky. Kinda dangerousical. Ain't too good if one of them things lands on your dopey noodle, 'specially from all the way up there."

"Must be wearing off," mumbled Ebegneeezer, glancing over at Dumpty and Humpty.

"Especially dangerousical if you're the lousy chicken," continued Gneeecey. "Their heads are awready kinda puny, y'know?"

"Wrong! Wrong! Wrong!" shouted Ebegneeezer. His supernatural eye clicked as it flashed rapidly.

I pinched Gneeecey's arm. He didn't notice. I sighed. He was going really loopy.

Frolicking in those floor vapors back in the mansion…not taking his meds…his worsening dimension burn…and now, because he was smaller than me, the Blobbert brothers' gelatin we'd unwittingly ingested had to be messing with his mind more than mine.

Cheek muscles twitching, Ebegneeezer placed a humongous glass bowl heaped with a jiggling purple mountain on his lookalike's lap. "I am convinced that sampling more of this delectable dessert would delight your taste buds."

Gneeecey's begrimed face lit up.

Luminous left eye still blazing, Ebegneeezer presented him with a small silver spoon.

The good diroctor raised his undersized implement, ready to dig in. "A little spoon makes the food bigger!" he shrieked, a grin plastered across his puss.

I leaped out of my chair and knocked the cheap piece of stainless steel out of his hand. "No, Diroctor! Don't! It messes with our minds! They want us to eat that, don'cha see, it came from *Humpty*!"

"We *shall* extract the truth from you two," declared Ebegneeezer, his orb shining on me. "You get orange. Dumpty just produced a fresh batch."

My muscles tensed.

"Gimmeee back my impooplement, ya lousy Ig!" whined Gneeecey. "Wha'cha stinkin' wanna doooo? Starve me to death?"

"You're not hungry, Diroctor! You just think you are. And they just wanna…they just wanna…"

Too late. Gneeecey plunged his salivating snout into the grape-flavored mess and gobbled it up. Defeated, I flopped back into my chair.

That moment, those jet engines began roaring in my head. Only saw that white haze. I squeezed my eyelids shut.

When they opened, Ebegneeezer stood motionless, his gesturing hands frozen in midair. Then, quite suddenly, he strode toward me, a smirk on his face.

Jerko still lay on the floor, a static grin spread across his ruddy face. Violet blobs dribbled from the good diroctor's long, outstretched tongue.

I wanted to yell Gneeecey's name, but my voice box wasn't functioning. I attempted to lunge in his direction, but couldn't move.

Only my eyeballs seemed capable of movement, and they must've grown to the size of golf balls as they rolled downward, to see my body constricted, shoulders to ankles, by a thin, translucent rope. A ghost of a rope.

Icy fear coursed through my veins.

Ebegneeezer pressed his face into mine. "Not such jolly fun when it happens to *you*, is it?"

"Yeah, Boss," bellowed Jerko as he came back to life. "She ain't laughin' *now*!"

My mouth was still on strike.

Ebegneeezer chuckled. "Enjoy your little waking nap, Earth girl."

Looked like I was just going to be a spectator.

"That is correct, Earth girl, you shall be a mere spectator," stated Ebegneeezer, reading my mind. "However, your turn *shall* come."

"That's what'cha get, ya lousy Ig, for tryin' to get us kilt again," Gneeecey hissed, through the side of his grape-stained snout.

I suddenly envisioned smacking Gneeecey upside his head. He winced and rubbed his dome. Encouraged that my powers might not be totally useless, I pictured shoving Jerko to the floor, just as he attempted to rise.

The gangster moaned. "Boss, can ya gimme a hand here?"

Ebegneeezer reached down to help him but fell forward and landed on his nose. It honked loudly. He raised his head and glared my way. If I could've moved, I would've shrugged. "You desire to play it like this, Earth girl? Have it your way, then." The translucent rope that bound my ribcage tightened. I could barely breathe.

"Alright, imposter," began Ebegneeezer, addressing his lookalike. "Substance certainly should have had enough time to work. And you have ingested a veritable ton of it. Now then, how do you know our Squigzy here?"

That very second, a gaunt, cucumber-headed man appeared. Gneeecey gasped. We knew him as the proprietor of Squiggleman's Hardware, back in Gneeecey's Perswayssick County.

"*Steve!*" shrieked Gneeecey. "*Steve Squiggleman!*"

Squigzy scrunched up his long bumpy nose like he smelled fish gone bad. "I don't know *you*." He glanced down at his tablet. "Never seen you in my life."

"But, I practically stinkin' *live* in your plumbin' store! I've even *pooped* there!"

"You must mean someone *else's* store," replied the sallow-skinned man, not even bothering to look up. "*I* don't have any store."

"But, of course ya do! Y'know, your store on Murgatroyd Avenue," Gneeecey insisted, his already high voice rising several octaves. "Bought all my stinkin' terlits from ya. Whole mansion's filled wit' 'em! Don'cha rememboober, your Mechanical Bull 2000? Your store model on display in your front window. It threw me when I tried to use it!"

Squigzy shot Ebegneeezer a "who is this guy?" look.

"So then ya felt bad an' gave me a discount on that fancy-schmancy Electronic Water Cyclone 3000! Y'know, three-thousan' cyclones per flush…"

"Enough!" shouted Ebegneeezer. "See, it is nonsense like this! How in Piggwinkle's wrinkled pink rump do you know Squigzy here?"

A glazy-eyed Gneeecey began nibbling up and down his right forearm. "To get to the other side of the road to comb the chicken's hair?"

Ebegneeezer smashed his fist on the desktop. "You are lying."

"No, I ain't," replied the good diroctor. His snout suddenly grew six inches.

"Alright, let us start from the beginning," suggested Ebegneeezer. "What is your name?"

"*Holy Saint Bogelthorpe!*" exclaimed Gneeecey, his crossed peepers glued to his muzzle as it expanded again, two whole feet.

"Liar!" bellowed Ebegneeezer. "What is your name?"

"Glad my pants ain't on fire," mumbled Gneeecey, watching his honker zoom out a yard's length.

"Wrong! What is your real name? Who *are* you?" demanded Ebegneeezer.

Gneeecey's eyes widened. "*Geewhizzicles!*"

"Wrong answer."

Gneeecey grasped his elongating nose. "Thought all of me stinkin' stopped growin'—years ago!"

"Evidently you did not."

"I *did*!" With that, the good diroctor's schnozz shot out several more yards and tumbled down into his lap, curling up neatly like a garden hose. A furry white garden hose.

Unable to speak, I could only gape.

Ebegneeezer shoved a pulsating blue rectangle into Squigzy's bony fingers. "Print me out three-thousand three-dimensional self-flushing toilets and install them in Shmuckettsville. At all of the coordinates designated in this report. At your earliest convenience."

"Sure thing, Boss. Right away."

"Additionally, investigate why the second sun's excess power is not simply being banked in our grid. It is downright tropical below in the underground car park."

"I'm on it, Boss."

Ebegneeezer turned his attention back to his fidgeting lookalike. "Alright. You do not know who you are. Perhaps that is unimportant. Where are you *from*, then?"

Gneeecey gawked at Squigzy. "*Three-dimensional printed-out terlits!*"

"You are deceiving us again," said Ebegneeezer. "There *is* no place called three-dimensional printed-out terlits."

Gneeecey's proboscis grew so long that the wet black tip with nostrils tumbled down to his ankles. "Oh, no! I don't wanna hafta smell my own stinkin' feet!"

Ebegneeezer chuckled. "Better you than me."

"You're messin' wit' our minds!" screamed Gneeecey. And with that, the good diroctor's overgrown beak, all fifteen yards of it, retracted back into his face like a metal tape measure snapping back into its dispenser. "Stinkin' *ooow!*"

-16-

UNLEASHING MY INNER GNEEECEY

THE TRANSLUCENT SNAKE that had bound me shattered as I propelled myself through the white haze of fury, smack into Ebegneeezer's face. Bits and pieces of the clear rope exploded into a zillion gleaming fragments as they hit the tiles.

Ebegneeezer's purple eye clicked like crazy, illuminating much of the room. Body rigid, his startled expression must've mirrored mine.

After about a minute he spoke. "Jerko, these two imposters shall come to regret their lack of forthrightness." He growled something under his breath about "not consistently being able to read that Earth girl's mind," then dashed out into the hallway.

"Gonna take care of them two," said Jerko, hot on his heels. "They're nuthin' but big trouble." The door slammed, and a lock turned.

Somehow, I was not afraid.

Gneeecey hopped off his stool. "Y'know, Ig, ya almos' got us kilt again."

I lowered myself back into my chair.

Gneeecey remained standing. "But, ya know what?"

"No, Diroctor. What?"

He cleared his throat. "This is gonna be igstremely difooficult for me to say, Ig."

Our eyes met.

He squirmed. "Uh, how do I stinkin' *say* this?"

"Say what?" I suddenly felt deflated. Didn't know whether it was exhaustion or relief.

"I'm, uh, well, really kinda proud of ya, Ig."

I sat up straight. "Huh?"

"Ya heard me, Ig. Don't make me say it no more or I might change my lousy mind."

My head tilted.

"I'm proud of ya for wha'cha jus' done," continued the canine-humanoid. "Ya unleashed your inner *meee*! Ya unleashed your inner *Gneeecey*!" He grinned.

"Why, um, thank you...I *think*." I wasn't quite convinced that unleashing my inner Gneeecey was necessarily a good thing.

"That's a severe compoopliment, Ig!"

"Yes, Diroctor. Uh-huh. Wow."

"Well, don't stinkin' say it so oogdimonious."

Hard not to be, well, oogdimonious. Anytime there was a quiet moment, my mind wandered back to my dimension. My family. My apartment. My job. My unpaid bills. And those disembodied eyeballs that might still be floating through my basement apartment. And poor Flea, trapped in my closet. I shuddered.

"Ya know, Ig," began Gneeecey, almost as if he had read my mind, "I know you're worried 'bout stuff back home. I stinkin' am, too. I got two, no make that three, places to worry 'bout."

Shifting in my seat, I nodded.

"There's my Planet Eccchs," he continued, "plus Perswayssick County…what a stinkin' mess I left *that* place in…an' there's my lovely new vehickookle, back in your dimension."

I groaned. That pastel black piece of rusted wreckage back home. The one that I had paid for.

"Sure hope Rico's friend's uncle-in-law's brother's cousin's dad don't take it back when they see I ain't been drivin' it."

"I wouldn't worry," I growled. "After all, it's been *paid* for."

The good director scratched his butt thoughtfully. "Ya know, Ig, if I ever get back my thousan'-dollar bill from them baaad kids that ain't mine, I might even *give* it to ya. Can't stinkin' believe I'm sayin' this, but it's the least I could do. I guess."

He shuffled over to me and put a grungy arm around my shoulder. "Ya know, Ig, lookin' back on it, I'm sure glad I didn't buy one of them garages or yards back in your dimension. I was real, real tempted. Saw signs for sales for both, all over your neighborhood."

-17-

THERE'S ALWAYS A WAY
...SOMETIMES

GNEEECEY'S GRIP TIGHTENED on the rusty prison bars. "Looky, Ig," he began, staring through our minuscule window, "ya better find a way to get us outta this stinkin' lousy mess ya got us into."

I rolled my eyes. "*I* got us into this mess? You're kidding, right?"

"Nope, I ain't, Ig. Ya did. An' you're gonna find a way to spring us outta here, y'know, before mornin', when that dopey other me imposter jerk says he's gonna throw us into that prison yard out there, full of all them killer zombies."

"Brains! Brains! We want brains!" chanted the walking dead in the courtyard below. "Grape brains! Orange brains! We love brains!"

Blinking, I rose from my thin straw bed. My shoeless feet almost cramped as I strode across the icy stone floor to join Gneeecey. True, if by daybreak we didn't supply Ebegneeezer with the wacky answers he demanded, we would end up down there, part of that mindless, milling mob.

I shivered, partly from the freezing air that blasted through the glassless opening and partly from the realization that we had no satisfactory responses for Ebegneeezer. His questions were nonsensical. Product of a paranoid mind. A mind that worked sort of like Gneeecey's. Two Gneeeceys…just my luck…to be imprisoned with one by another. I could only pray that there weren't any more of 'em out there in the universe. Or freakin' multiverse.

It was not a pretty sight down below. The two setting suns cast long shadows in the courtyard. Perfect lighting for a horror movie set. Unfortunately, this was no movie. My stomach did flip flops as I stood watching, transfixed.

The gothic-style black iron gate creaked open, seemingly by itself. Seconds later, a chubby, gray-haired man lumbered through. He pushed a humongous wheelbarrow heaped with orange and purple gelatin brains.

I leaned my elbows on the rocky window sill, quickly removing them as arrows of pain darted up into my shoulders.

The chants below intensified as the inmates lumbered toward the old man.

Unfazed, he began tossing the colorful organs to them. One bounced into the soiled hands of a stooped-over woman whose white hair zigzagged out of her scalp like lightning bolts. "*Ooooh, braaains,*" she moaned, eyes glazed with greed.

Another, a zebra-humanoid, snatched a tangerine blob from the pile and crammed it into his mouth, whole. Fragments glistened, reflecting the blood red sunset as they sprayed from his busy jaws. Spying us, he grinned and waved. "Hi, guys! Ya might know my twin brother! He drives a cab!"

"Yeah…stinkin' whatever." Gneeecey waved back halfheartedly, then plunged both fists into the pockets of the baggy navy trousers he had been forced to wear. Still garbed in NickNick's feathered atrocity, I just sighed.

The din died down as the zombies began chomping. Soon all you could hear was the slobbering. I had to look away.

Gneeecey shot me a "told you so" look. "Well, Ig, wha'cha gotta say *now?*"

Our eyes met. "There's always a way," I mumbled. "*Sometimes.*"

My heart nearly stopped when a sudden pounding shook our thick wooden door.

-18-

THERE ARE HUNGRY PEOPLE ON
OTHER PLANETS

"A hungry man will eat boiled shoe leather."
Salvador F. Solá, M.D.

M Y OVERWORKED TICKER POUNDED through my ribcage as the hulking figure barged into our gloomy dungeon.

Dim lighting from the corridor revealed the intruder to be Jerko. Amber complexion glowing supernaturally, exactly like that of his evil lookalike from Gneeecey's dimension, blond big-nosed Mark, he flung a couple of trays in our direction. Food flew all over the place as the aluminum skidded along the stone floor. "Ain't paid to be no waitress," muttered the gangster.

"Heh, heh, bad evenin'. Uh, whazzup?" The tremble in Gneeecey's voice belied his attempt to sound casual.

"Bad evenin' yourself. Real bad evenin'. Ain't nuthin' up. Except possibly my time workin' this stupid job." Kicking aside bits of spilled chow, Jerko lumbered across the cell and pointed his sausage of an index finger at the window. "Remember, youse two ain't gonna get nice meals like this no more if youse don't play nice. You'll be down there whinin' wit' the rest of them ZomSect3 zombies if youse don't come up wit' the right answers by the time them two suns come up."

"But...but," spluttered Gneeecey, nibbling on his wrist, "we can't think of no right answers..."

"Ain't *my* problem," growled Jerko as he stormed out. "Sick of stuff always bein' *my* problem." He slammed the door shut and latched us in.

"I jus' don't stinkin' *understaaand*!" wailed Gneeecey, addressing the crudely crafted wooden door.

"Me either, Diroctor." I dropped down to my knees to take a closer look at dinner. The rectangular platters contained a few puny pieces of what appeared to be sloppily buttered burned toast, surrounded by small black spheres (possibly overdone green peas), and surprisingly unbroken glass dessert cups heaped with orange and purple jelled mini-brains.

"Don't even *think* of eating those brains," I warned.

Gneeecey glanced down, snout crinkled. "Lousy toast looks kinda cold."

"Diroctor, if you happen to see any microwaves here in this freakin' medieval prison, please do inform me."

"Y'know, that reminds me of another thing I gotta mention, Ig," squeaked Gneeecey, his already high voice tightening. "Never brung it up before, but I noticed when ya stayed wit' me in my mansion, ya wasted lotsa food. Repoopeatedly."

I sprang up. "What?"

"Ig," he continued, as if addressing a clueless toddler, "when ya put a plate in the stinkin' microwave, you're supposed to eat that, too! Sheeesh. There are hungry people on other planets!"

"Diroctor, our nerves are shot. We're in big trouble. We really don't need to be arguing with each other."

He stared down at his sneakers.

A sudden rustling of wings startled us.

"Stinkin' Mister Gobblesnotts!" Fists waving, Gneeecey fell back onto one of the food trays. His butt honked loudly.

The white-and-black checkered guinea pig sat perched on the window sill, staring our way. A flat, round silver object about three inches in diameter sparkled from between his teeth.

As Gneeecey shot up and lunged toward him, the critter flapped away into the night. "What's wrong wit' that flyin' rat?"

"You scared him away!"

Before Gneeecey could open his yapper, Mister Gobblesnotts returned and settled back on the ledge, that gleaming mystery object still in his mouth. I tiptoed over to him. "Mister Gobblesnotts," I said softly, "nice of you to come pay us a visit in this, uh, place. What brings you here?"

Ebony eyes widening, the guinea pig twisted his head sideways and slid his treasure between the iron bars, right into my fingers. For the first time in many moons, make that many suns, I smiled.

Mister Gobblesnotts appeared to smile back. I held NickNick's car in the palm of my hand.

Stuffing the precious disk into my outfit's single fluff-edged pocket, I crouched down and plucked a piece of toast off one of the food trays. When I offered the furry creature a crispy triangle, he extended his two tiny paws, snatched the snack and fluttered away.

Gneeecey rushed toward the window. "Ya stinkin' gave that flyin' rat my lousy dinner!"

I shook my head. "No, I didn't. You *sat* on yours."

The good diroctor turned to inspect his tray. Plastered to his cotton-covered behind were two slices of bread, (buttered sides up, of course), flanked by clumps of squished orange and purple mini-brains.

-19-

CONFOOFIDENTIALLY SPEAKIN'

I G," GNEEECEY BLEATED from across the blackness of our cell, "I caaan't stinkin' fall asleeeeep."

"Me either." Unable to sleep myself, ready to crawl out of my skin, I pulled what felt like a porcupine blanket up around my shaking shoulders.

"We gotta talk, Ig."

I bolted upright, knocking some nearby metallic object to the stone floor.

"Whassamatter, Ig?"

Swore I saw a tiny light blink up above us. I shook my head. Had to be impossible in such a medieval dungeon. Must've been a hallucination.

"I *said*, whassamatter, Ig?"

"Director, did you see a red flash just a second ago? Up over our heads?"

"Nah, Ig. An' *I'm* the one who usually sees weird junk. Y'know, 'cause of my lousy Redecoritis. Stinkin' neurologikookal impairment. Before, I did think that ol' busticated wood chair in here was starin' at me all kinda funny, but now it's dark, so it ain't botherin' me all that much."

My heart sank, remembering that he didn't have his meds with him.

"Almost stinkin' slapped the lousy chair."

"Diroctor, you're sure you don't have your meds somewhere in that big shirt pocket of yours?"

"Nope, checked sevooveral times. Ain't got 'em. Like we say on my planet, too bad, three eggs. Y'know, mayboobee *yooou* need 'em if you're seein' stuff that proboobably ain't there."

I mumbled something that even I didn't understand.

"We got a real proboobblem here."

"Yes, Diroctor." I shifted onto my side and leaned on my elbow, monitoring the ceiling, relieved each moment that I didn't detect another scarlet flicker above. "Y'know, this freakin' prickly straw bed is even worse than that mutant spring-popping mini-mattress I slept on when I stayed in your mansion."

"Stinkin' whatever. But that was then an' this is now."

"True that. But my back still hasn't recovered from those three months."

"Uh-huh. Yeah. Heya, Ig…"

"The name would be *Nicki*."

"Yeah. Okay, Ig. I wanna know somethin'. Did ya really mean it, back in your place, when ya said ya were worried 'bout me? Y'know, before ya saw me again?"

I could just about make out Gneeecey's fidgeting form. "You mean, when I mentioned that I was worried about what happened to you after we left that weird ice crystal dimension we were trapped in, where there was no up or down?"

"Wasn't no gravoovity neitherwise."

"Yep….and I don't know whether to tell you *this* or not…"

112

"Tell me, Ig, tell me!"

I cleared my throat. "Diroctor, I've been…well…struggling with something…I'm having real problems remembering certain things. Ever since I reentered my own world, there are, like…these empty spaces in my memory, half-remembered things…it's been driving me crazy."

"Perhaphoops it's jus' dimension burn?"

"That would be logical. When you reappeared in my dimension, all these memories came flooding back. I remembered being in the ice crystal haze and how that monster of an invisible force separated us at about five-zillion miles an hour. And when it catapulted me back into my dimension, how at first I was really worried about what happened to you. But then I totally forgot until you appeared the other night."

"But ya were worried?"

"Yes."

"Thanks, Ig." I imagined him to be grinning.

"And *please*," I began, making no attempt to hide my exasperation, "feel free to call me by my actual name, the one assigned to me at birth. *Nicki*."

"Okay, Ig."

I sighed. Once an Ig, always an Ig…I guess.

"Ig…"

"*Yessss?*"

"This is kinda like that time, ain't it? I mean, there *is* gravoovity here, but it's stinkin' cold, an' we don't really know which way is which, or what's gonna hapoopen to us."

As if I couldn't feel any colder, an extra chill sliced through my bones.

"Ig, I'm nervoovous. Usually, I got a lousy answer for every stinkin' question. Y'know?"

"Yes," I replied, through chattering teeth. "I know."

"Ig…in case we don't, y'know, never see each other again after them two suns come up 'cause we don't give 'em the right answers, I wanna tell ya 'bout somethin'."

"Yeah, sure."

"Confoofidentially speakin', of course."

"Of course." I winced as the anguished, prolonged groan of a lone zombie echoed in the courtyard below. Maybe they had nightmares, too.

"Never told no one else 'bout this, not even Fleaglossity," continued Gneeecey. "Could ruin my prekookarious pollutical standin' back home. An' my whole *life*." He paused. "Now, for some stinkin' reason, I trust ya. An' I really need to get this off of my chest."

"Okay." I felt oddly touched.

"Ya rememboober I mighta mentioned to ya that I worked my way through medical school back on Planet Eccchs?"

I nodded out of habit, even though I knew he couldn't see me. "Uh-huh."

"Well, I was a junior clerk. In our local Office of Threes. Y'know how valuable a three is, where I'm from. An' to think, they entrusticated *meee* wit' 'em, even though I was so young."

"Yes, Diroctor, you did mention that once or twice."

"Well, I never told you or no one else what hapoopened…"

Shivering uncontrollably, I drew my itchy blanket up around my neck.

"There were all kinds of threes," he continued. "Blue threes, green threes, plaaastic threes, wooden threes, metal threes, an' paper an' cardboard threes. Some were even three glonkometers long, that's 'bout a quarter of a foot, in youse Earth people's more, uh, primitive measurements."

"What exactly was your job there?" I inquired, ignoring his last snarky remark.

"I was supposed to sepooparate the threes by size, color, an' material, an' y'know, enter 'em into the inventory computer. Then lock 'em all up in this gigantical vault." He paused.

"And?"

"Well, Ig, this here is the confoofidential part. Sometimes a paper or cardboard *eight* was turned in…they were very rare. *Twice* as valuable." He took a deep, snorting breath. "An', instead of loggin' 'em in…I would…well…I would…"

"You would what?"

His shrill voice morphed into a whisper. "I would stinkin' take these big scissors an' cut the lousy eights in half…when I thought no one was lookin'…an' I'd pocket a three. Each time."

"You get caught?"

After a prolonged silence, he continued. "My supoopervisor, Mister Forkworthy, he knowed me a long time 'cause his wife Missus Forkworthy was my firs' grade teacher, she had yellow hair an' I did good wit' her 'cause she always seemed to call on me whenever the answer was three."

"That certainly was lucky."

"Yeah, Ig, it most certaintaneously was. Anyways, to lengthen a short story, one day Mister Forkworthy says to me, 'Son, I got eyes in the back of my head an' they been glued to ya for weeks. I should really fire ya an' inform the authorities, but I jus' can't bring myself to. I knowed ya for such a long time, since ya were knee-high to a glompershprout, an' I always seen so many good qualities in ya. Real potential.'"

"So," I interjected, convinced that despite the darkness, I could see the grayish vapor of my own breath, "he gave you another chance?"

"Yeah, Ig. He held out this gigantical wood box an' tol' me to empty all my pockets. An' I did. Filled up that whole box, plus another. Blue threes, green threes, paper an' cardboard threes, an' even a purpoople three. Also, some plaaastic threes an' even a three from this wooden eight I managed to split, wit' great difooficulty, of course, hidin' under my desk."

"You kept your job?"

"Yeah, Ig. Through the rest of medical school. Mister Forkworthy warned me that fatefootful day, 'Young Bizzig, I'll see ya here again tomorrow afternoon, but don't lemme *never* catch ya embezoozlin' another three.' Can't say I wasn't tempted at times, 'specially when a beaudiful shiny gold or red eight would show up. But I kep' my promise. Never cut up another eight or pocketed another three."

I exhaled deeply. "Wow, lucky you had such an understanding and compassionate boss—one who really believed in you."

"Yeah, Ig. Hey, y'don't suppose that now this here is all punishment for what I done back then?"

"You mean karma?"

"Nah, Ig. We ain't discussin' automobiles. An' I ain't your mom. I stinkin' mean, do ya think I'm in this here bad situation 'causa what I done back then?"

"No, Diroctor. And remember, *I'm* here in this situation with you as well."

"Yeah, ya are. Ya think we're here 'causa somethin' *yooou* done?"

"No, I really don't…"

A loud swishing by the window interrupted me. I leaped up. Nothing to see, except for the silhouette of bars.

"*Well, Ig?*" asked Gneeecey, his voice cracking.

"Nothing there." My heart fluttered as I flopped back onto my pile of straw and hid underneath my blanket.

"What're we gonna do in the mornin', Ig, when them two suns stinkin' come up, an' that other lousy me imposter asks us all them crazy questions that ain't really questions 'cause they ain't really got answers?"

"Diroctor, we're just gonna have to try and answer his crazy questions the best we can. That's all any of us can do at the end of a day. The best we can."

"Yeah, Ig. An' it *is* the end of a day."

-20-

MISTER PHORTYPHARTS SHALL RECORD YOUR TESTIMONY

THE TWO SUNS BLAZED through the high windows illuminating the otherwise gloomy corridor. Out in the courtyard, restless zombies moaned and shuffled about, anxious for breakfast no doubt.

Jerko muttered a stream of unintelligible syllables at our backs as he marched Gneeecey and me to the interrogation room, our wrists handcuffed together. Felt like we'd been trudging along like that for miles.

"Wait here." The gangster stopped to confer with a uniformed officer whose sharp chin immediately jutted in our direction. Badge identifying him as Guard No. 36, the man growled something at his five charges, bound together with manacles, a middle-aged blond man and woman, a handsome dark-skinned black man looking to be in his late twenties, and two older redheaded pink-faced women who, except for a sizable difference in height, looked like twins. Lined up against the cinderblock wall with faces hardened, they all glared at Gneeecey and me. Strangely, each one looked familiar.

"Well, *look* who karma has come to bite," said the larger sister, her husky voice tinged with sarcasm.

Her shorter, identically dressed lookalike laughed. "A welcome sight."

"You bet," chimed in the young man, standing tall. "What goes around comes around."

"True, Clyde," replied the other man. "Always. Right, Meg?"

"Yep, honey." The golden-haired woman looked daggers at us. "Evidently someone sold *them* out. Just like they did *us*."

Gneeecey's yapper opened wide. My jaw dropped.

* * *

EBEGNEEEZER MOTIONED TO GNEEECEY, who sat on a tiny wooden chair, kicking his red high tops nervously. "You *do* realize that everything you say can and shall be used against you?"

Before Gneeecey could reply, I leaped out of my little school chair, complete with attached desk, nearly knocking it over. "Hey! That's not *fair*! That's not how it *goes*!"

Ebegneeezer strode across the fluorescent-lit office, pushed me back into my seat and jammed his face into mine. "You are not under oath and therefore shall not be taken seriously."

"I will not be treated like this!"

Ebegneeezer crossed his arms. His purple gaze settled on me, causing me to squint. "Your turn may come, but probably not, as we have sufficient evidence that proves that your memory is faulty and thereby of little use."

My face flushed. "*What* evidence?"

119

"Suffice it to say, a little birdie enlightened us concerning your dubious mental status. Mister Phortypharts, old fellow, please strike her comments from the record."

"Yes, Your Royal Grate Hynesty," replied a forty-something skeleton of a man, bony fingers tapping out a staccato rhythm on the keys of a stenography machine. His tan lapels were stained with brown muck that matched his greasy thinning hair.

Ebegneeezer handed Gneeecey a clipboard and a green neon pen that resembled a narrow test tube. A nib protruded from its rounded end. "You do realize that this is your final opportunity to be truthful. Now, fill this out. At once!"

"Asks here where I'm stinkin' from," said Gneeecey, hands and voice shaking. "Awready tol' youse, I'm originally from Planet Eccchs. To be more specifoofic, my dad's family's from Dorkyville, so I'm actually part Dorkish."

"Don't tell me. Simply write it all down on the form."

Gneeecey scratched his butt thoughtfully. "Whuddabout this dopey part here, asks for necks of skin?"

Ebegneeezer tapped his shiny oxford impatiently. "That would be next of kin."

"Hmm…lemme think…uh…"

Lower lip curled with contempt, Ebegneeezer glanced my way. "Just list *her* as your next of kin. It is solely a formality. It is not likely to matter by the time we get through with the both of you, old chap."

"Okaysickles…I guess…necks of skin, the Ig."

Ebegneeezer snatched the paper and studied it for a second or two. "Completely implausible."

Gneeecey sat up straight. "Ain't implausibooble. Hapoopens to be the lousy unfalse truth."

His lookalike shook his head. "It's all flubdub to me."

"Ya know my...uh...stinkin' frenemy, *Flubbubb?*"

"I said *flubdub.*"

"Oh. Thought'cha said *Flubbubb.* He ain't here an' I don't think ya know him. But unfortunatively, *I* do. Stinkin' grew up together."

Ebegneeezer's eyes rolled up to the ceiling, then down to Gneeecey's document.

"Alright...uh...*Dirrector* Gneeecey, Mister Phortypharts shall record your testimony, which automatically puts you under solemnly sworn oath."

With that, Gneeecey fell off his chair and onto his nose, which honked loudly. "Stinkin' *ow!*"

The stenographer clacked away as I rushed over to help the good dirrector to his feet.

With great fanfare, Ebegneeezer cleared his throat. "Mister Phortypharts, strike out the nasal honk and also the 'stinkin' ow' part, please."

"Yes, Your Grate Royal Hynesty."

Regaining his composure, Gneeecey trudged back to his seat. Emboldened, he addressed his lookalike. "Ya know, I've come to the concussion that you're proboobably jus' a figment of my imagination."

"Most likely, you have *had* a concussion, you daft fool."

"Are ya stinkin' tryin' to say I need psykookiatric help? I'll have ya know..."

"Take it whatever way you want, you blithering pea brain."

"Serialistically," continued Gneeecey, "I don't appreciate your snarkasm, your lousy blamestormin' or your vindictful bossdom. Plus, ya talk real funny."

"So do you." Ebegneeezer raised an eyebrow as he handed the good dirrector a yellow pad.

"Next, we shall evaluate your questionable cognitive function. Please complete this most basic mathematical test. Then we shall review those questions you failed to answer previously."

Gneeecey scribbled something, then two seconds later tossed the test at the desk. "This dopey mathemetratical test is simpoople. Ain't nuthin' wrong wit' my stinkin' cognoonitive function."

Snout crinkled, Ebegneeezer snatched the paper. "Blimey! Half of eight is not *three*!"

"Is where *I* stinkin' come from," replied Gneeecey, voice crackling with defiance.

"We shall see, we shall see. Now step over here and empty the contents of your T-shirt pocket upon this desk. Perhaps then we shall make some sense of all of this utter nonsense before we return to those other critically important questions."

I bolted upright. "You can't make him…"

"It's awright, Ig, ain't got nuthin' to hide…in my shirt pockooket, anyways. Ain't nuthin' here to impooplicate me or damage my fine repoopootation."

Sighing, I slumped back in my chair. It would be best to keep quiet, lest I be forced to empty my outfit's one pocket that contained NickNick's stolen car.

The moment I thought of my lookalike, her head popped through a rear doorway. "Processing papers for them and the next group are all prepared and ready to sign, my dear, wonderful, awesome boss."

"Ugh," I muttered, nose wrinkled.

"Thank you, my little Igglett," replied Ebegneeezer, eyes on the good diroctor.

She smirked at me and disappeared.

It took forever-and-a-half for Gneeecey to empty his T-shirt pocket. Piled up on Ebegneeezer's desktop were a partially eaten slice of pizza, a thick Perswayssick County phone book, a half-shattered wooden gavel, an aquamarine "BZZG" monogrammed junior bowling ball, a box of Freak O'Nature Health Cigars that the good diroctor depended upon to counteract his chronic constipation, plus what appeared to be a chewed up violin, a pair of aviator sunglasses, an outer slide tube he carried just in case he ever encountered a trombone missing that very same part, a dirty red sneaker, a pocket toilet plunger, his gold earring, and a small silver frame.

"Oh, an' *looky*!" cried Gneeecey as he lobbed a clear blue container at his mountain of belongings. "I stinkin' had my lousy meds the whole time! Forgot they were in this dopey dispenser Flea gave me! Stooopid Fleaglossity, always makin' my life so incornvenient!"

I blinked. Each time I heard Flea's name, I was haunted by some murky half-dream where the grimacing superhero was begging me to do something. Had no idea what.

Ebegneeezer whisked away the little plastic pill receptacle. Two other items had caught his eye, the plunger, "Squiggleman Hardware" engraved on its wooden handle, and particularly, the framed photograph of Goonafina. He smashed both fists on the desk so forcefully that the good diroctor's possessions flew off, in all directions. "This bloody interrogation has certainly raised more questions than it has answered!"

"Can we go home, then?" inquired Gneeecey, as he scooped his personal effects up off the floor and crammed them back into his pocket. "Aboobsolutely gotta get back to my Perswayssick County for F-Day!"

"Yes, you may go home," replied Ebegneeezer, gray clouds of smoke actually billowing from his ears. "You shall both reside in your *new* home until we sort this all out...the ZomSect3 courtyard, a gated community where you shall doubtless enjoy your lives among the living dead, and assimilate rather quickly, I might add."

-21-

PLEASE DON'T EAT THE BRAINS

THE JIGGLING GELLED BRAINS glistened in the moonlight as the wheelbarrow that transported them wobbled down the cobblestones, swarmed by hordes of hungry zombies.

"Diroctor," I warned, "please don't even *think* of eating any of those."

"No worries, Ig. Ain't got much crappetite tonight."

"Me either. Stomach's actually killing me. And it's freakin' *freezin'* out here."

"What're we stinkin' gonna *dooo*? All them spooky spiked black iron gates surroundicatin' this place look way too tall to climb over. Too dangerousical to even try." Shivering himself, Gneeecey collapsed onto a bumpy cement bench.

I sat down beside him. "Don't know what we're gonna do. And I wonder, do these, uh, *people* ever sleep? Doesn't even look like there's anywhere to lay down, except for maybe these few miserable seats."

"Y'know, Ig, them zomboobies don't look like the regoogoolar kind of undead ya see in all the movies. They ain't fallin' apart an' rottin' alive or nuthin'. Or scoopin' people's brains out wit' shovels an' spoons." With that, he yanked that partially eaten slice of pizza out of his T-shirt pocket and began nibbling noisily. "Want some, Ig? Extra cheese! Aged cross-eyed cheese wit' petrified pepooperoni!"

"Uh…no thanks. And I thought you said you weren't hungry."

"Wasn't, till I started smellin' all them fruity brains over there. Orange an' grape. Yum!"

The icy slab we sat on felt like extra coarse sandpaper on steroids. It promised to be a long night. All I needed was for Gneeecey to ingest one of those quivering blobs, then go even loopier on me. "You know, Diroctor, you're right. These are not regular zombies. Don't you remember what happened to us during that first cross-examination? When they made us say that the red parrot was blue, even though we knew he wasn't?"

"Yeah, Ig. I do rememboober."

"They put that wacko gunk that Dumpty and Humpty produce into those dessert bowls and flavored brains, so they can freakin' try to control people's minds."

"Yeah, Ig."

"So please don't eat the brains!"

Grimacing, Gneeecey shimmied closer to me as one of our new neighbors began to wail, loud enough to wake the dead.

Despite the arctic air and sporadic screams, we dozed off, awakening just as several shadowy figures approached. As they came closer, I recognized them as the five prisoners that had taunted us earlier, on our way to the interrogation room.

"Hey, you two," called out the young six-footer whose facial features were so finely chiseled—and oddly familiar. I remembered that his name was Clyde.

Gneeecey and I bolted upright. "Uh-oh," he muttered, "more stinkin' troubooble!"

"We want to apologize," began the blond woman. "We honestly thought you were *them*. But now we know that you couldn't possibly be." Her tone was gentle.

The good diroctor and I rose.

"Name's Meg. Meg Shipman," continued the lady, adding, "this is my husband, Brad." Smiling, he nodded our way.

"And I'm Clyde Weaver. Sorry for the way we treated you. We honestly thought you were *them*."

"We sure did. I'm Vlatta Velm, and I want you to meet my younger twin, Velma Vlatt. We both do apologize," said the taller sister. "Profusely."

"Youse mus' be fraternical twins," observed Gneeecey, head tilted. "Youse two ain't the same size."

"But we're doubly wise," said Velma. The sturdy redheads, probably in their sixties, sported unusual identical navy business suits consisting of horizontally pin-striped blazers and skirts. Sleek white sneakers, decorated with silver lightning bolts, adorned their feet.

Gneeecey and I exchanged handshakes with our latest acquaintances. "I'm Nicki Rodriguez, and this is…"

"I can introducerate my stinkin' self," snapped Gneeecey. "*I* am Diroctor B.Z.Z. Gneeecey, Grate Gizzygalumpaggis an' also Quality of Life Commissioner of Perswayssick County, plus CEO of the GAS Broadcast Network. An' also Gneeezles Restaurant, where our slogan is, 'Who sez good food has to be good?'" He paused for a moment. "I'm originally from consonant-rich Planet Ecccchs—three Cs, a H an' a S, but'cha pronounciate 'em like a X. Y'know what they say, Eccchs marks the spot!"

"I'm from Earth," I continued. "Diroctor Gneeecey was, uh, visiting my dimension, and somehow the two of us landed here. At first, we thought we were back in his dimension, but I quickly came to the conclusion that we somehow ended up in a parallel universe."

"Most probable explanation," agreed Clyde, running a hand over his head of closely cropped black hair. "We absolutely couldn't believe our eyes when we saw you two out in that corridor, coming and going, before we were brought in to *them*. Your lookalikes."

I absolutely couldn't believe my eyes. Clyde was an exact double of Cleve Wheeler, a dear friend I'd made back in Perswayssick County. A GAS Network co-worker. Never got to go out on that dinner date to celebrate my birthday, or make that trip downtown to Murgatroyd Music to finally buy the guitar he'd put on layaway. Too much crazy stuff had gotten in our way. And crazy people too, including Gneeecey. During my whole extended misadventure in Perswayssick County, Cleve had made me forget about Carlos...*Cleve* was the nameless, elusive figure who had been lurking in the recesses of my mind...haunting me...until now. Standing right in front of me was...

"That's right!" agreed Meg, rousing me from my reverie as she slowly lowered herself onto a flat, cragged rock. "Couldn't believe it!"

I pointed to the bench we had occupied. "Please, sit down. It's not all that comfortable, but it's gotta be better than that boulder."

"Thanks, it's okay," replied Meg. "We're kind of used to roughing it." She and her husband, attired in matching maroon sweats, exchanged amused glances. The couple, whom I knew I'd seen somewhere before, appeared to be in their mid-forties and exceptionally fit. Six-foot-six, Brad's thinning blond hair went silver at his temples, and honey, shoulder-length hair framed his considerably shorter wife's flawless complexion. Close up, their eyes, his emerald, and hers gray conveyed a deep sadness.

"Y'know," began Gneeecey, addressing Clyde, "I got this guy, Cleve Wheeler, workin' for me at my GAS Broadcast Network, back in my Perswayssick County. Ya look an' sound 'zactly like him." The good diroctor shot me a sideways glance. "Good friend of the Ig here, too. Too stinkin' much of a good friend."

I bit my tongue.

"An' youse two," continued Gneeecey, gaping at Brad and Meg, "look 'zactly like Burt an' Mary. Owners of Shisskey's Bakery, where I go every mornin' for my whooped cream thingy, y'know, wit' that lousy yummy cherry on top? Youse guys are on Murgatroyd Avenue, near Squiggleman's Hardware where I buy all my terlits, an' ol' Gus's Sock Repair Shop. Brung some of my busted socks there las' week. Not to get 'em cleaned, jus' fixed."

Meg and Brad seemed to be struggling to keep straight faces.

The good diroctor turned to the sisters. "An' youse two, you're 'zact dupooplicates of our twins, county freeloader Vlotta Vern an' city council troublemaker Verna Vlott. Difooferent heights like youse guys, an' born on difooferent days. Youse two talk in rhymes, too. Mus' be related to Ol' Mother Goose. Or Ol' Mother Hubbard. An' youse both gave me a real bad time at that las' Quality of Life meetin', too. Lotsa pollutical problems."

Giggling, Vlatta and Velma shrugged.

"Parallel universe is the only plausible explanation here," stated Clyde.

Head spinning, I had to sit down. Gneeecey hopped back onto the bench as well.

The two sisters plopped themselves down alongside us. "So, tell me," began the good director, pointing at me, "what did that stinkin' evil other meee an' that lousy, horribooble other her do to youse fine peopoople?"

"To make a long story short," replied Clyde, stooping down low as he addressed Gneeecey, "your dastardly doubles betrayed us…"

Suddenly, two hulking figures were looming over us. Gneeecey sprang into my lap.

"Bwaaa haaa haaa haaa!" bellowed Dumpty and Humpty, bouncing up and down.

"Just stopping by to check on our newest inmates," Dumpty informed us.

"And we personally want to make sure that you all eat!" added Humpty as he displayed a humongous platter heaped with purple and orange brains. "You don't want to make us feel bad. Wouldn't be very polite. Or smart."

"Well, I pride myself on not bein' stinkin' polite, but I *aaam* smart," replied the good diroctor. "Igstremely smart. So, I guess a brain or two would proboobably only make me more smarter, if that was even possibooble."

I tightened my arms around Gneeecey's shoulders.

"Stop! Get offa me, ya lousy Ig!"

I stared Humpty's way. "You're wasting your time. We're not gonna eat these."

"Yeah, man," agreed Clyde, nose wrinkled like he smelled an overflowing sewer. "Ain't gonna indulge. Sorry, but not sorry."

With that, Humpty plucked an orange brain off the plate and flung it in Clyde's face. I leaped up. "That's *it!* You think you can just go around disrespecting people?" Jet engines roared between my ears as that milky haze obliterated everything except the outlines of the two oval blobs. Muscles tensed, I concentrated my sights on them. "How dare you mess with people's minds? Well, I bet you freakin' won't anymore!"

I stared through narrowed lids until steam sizzled from both eggs. Seconds later, the Blobbert Brothers dissolved into two ginormous puddles.

Gneeecey's jaw dropped. "*Ig, ya stinkin' kilt 'em!*"

The seven of us sprinted toward the entrance to escape the mindless feeding frenzy that followed as throngs of our fellow inmates, humanoids, canine-humanoids, and Mister ZeeBee's zebra-humanoid twin, dropped onto their hands and knees to slurp up the orange and purple pools that had overspread the courtyard.

As I leaned up against the fence to catch my breath, some squeaky, distressed cries caught my attention. I staggered over to the gate and crouched down.

"Looky, Ig!" shouted Gneeecey, running up behind me. "It's Mister Gobblesnotts!"

Crammed into a tiny wire cage, the checkered critter was unable to even raise his head. My blood pressure rose as I read the note attached to the handle. *Gatekeeper, as per His Royal Grate Hynesty's orders, please dispose of this filthy creature at your earliest convenience. Thanking you in advance, His Grate Royal Hynesty's Assigned Representative, NickNick.*

"Ain't *even* gonna happen." I ripped the tag off and handed it to Meg, who muttered something as she knelt down beside me. Clyde, Brad, Vlatta, and Velma shook their heads as they gathered around.

I glanced over at Meg. "We've gotta get this poor little guy out."

She lifted a lever. "I work with an animal rescue in my spare time. We routinely use these catch and release traps." She snapped the prison portal open, and the grateful guinea pig scrambled out. He headbutted the two of us, much as a cat would.

"Fly away, Mister Gobblesnotts, please," I said, stroking his furry noggin. "Don't *ever* go back home! Be *free*! And thank you, for *everything*!" The way he gazed up at me convinced me that he'd understood all I'd said.

Appearing to wink, he soared up into the night sky wings spread, visible against the silvery full moon.

* * *

GNEEECEY REACHED UP and tapped Clyde's kneecap. "Gonna tell us what them lousy stinkin' evil lookalikes did to youse guys, before them two suns come up?"

Clyde sighed. "Like I started to say, before we were so rudely interrupted, your doubles sold us out." He pulled a shiny disk out of the pocket of his gray sweats. "See this? Brad, Meg and I are the scientists who invented this high-tech vehicle."

Gneeecey's peepers widened. "Wowzickles! *Youse* guys *invented* 'em?"

"At the request of the government," continued Clyde. "Ebegneeezer Eeeceygnay himself commissioned us. Promised we'd share in the profits, which he guaranteed would be spectacular."

"That's where my sister and I came in," said Velma, buttoning up her blazer to keep warm. "Our job was to seek and secure extra funding for the project, at Ebegneeezer's request. And we did. Worked really hard."

"But," chimed in Vlatta, "up his sleeve, Ebegneeezer had a card."

Jogging in place, Brad chuckled. "Yep, the five of us left good jobs to work on this whole thing."

"So, Cleve, I mean Clyde, what 'zactly hapoopened?"

"We were totally discredited. Eeeceygnay claimed that *he* invented the vehicle, and then he fired us. Only thing we got out of it was ulcers. Guess that's what our Grate BigButtKizz means when he tells us he gives us the shirts off our backs."

"Wowzickles! Even *I* stinkin' wouldn't do *thaaat*! An' whuddabout the lousy Ig's doubooble?"

"Industrial spy. Copied schematics and other classified info. Cooked the books, too. Told backers that the project was a complete failure and suggested they write it off as a loss. Showed 'em falsified documents.

And how would anyone know? Only she and Eeeceygnay possess these vehicles." Clyde paused and winked. "And *us*. Only three were ever produced. On *this* planet, anyway. The five of us share it."

I pulled NickNick's car out of my pocket. "And thanks to Mister Gobblesnotts, my evil, absolutely disgusting lookalike is missing hers."

Clyde's ebony eyes settled on me. "She even came on to me. And at first, I went for her. I'm sure that enabled her to access info…my fault to even give her that opening. Stupid of me."

Despite the frigid air, my blood was boiling.

Brad stood still for a moment. "Don't be so hard on yourself, Clyde. When we're straight up with people, we expect the same from them."

"We all made mistakes," said Vlatta. "Even my sis and I fell for NickNick's sob stories, how she was bullied and mistreated by Ebegneeezer."

"I'm not a geezer, but old enough certainly," added Velma, "to realize her stories had a bad smell."

Vlatta sighed. "In our heads should've rung a loud bell."

Meg pulled her hood up over her head. "I was sympathetic, too."

"Anyway," concluded Clyde, "we're all discredited and out of work. Living off savings and doing odd jobs. And now we're here."

Meg nodded.

Brad kicked a small rock. "And Ebegneeezer and NickNick are profiting from sales of this vehicle on Gnauzea Three, a planet in our twin sun's solar system."

"Nice soundin' name for a planet, I gotta say," remarked Gneeecey, sneaking a bite of pizza from his T-shirt pocket.

"We're *here* 'cause we won't just go away," said Meg. "We know too much."

Brad crossed his arms. "And we have no intentions of going away. We'll get justice. One way or another."

"I know this much," I began, barely able to hear my own voice through the roaring in my skull, "they are *not* gonna win *this* one." Fists clenched, I concentrated on the black iron fence until two pickets heated up red and bent, just wide enough to squeeze through.

One by one, we slid through and scattered, leaving the kneeling, still slurping zombies to themselves.

-22-

GOTTA THINK LIKE AN ECCCHSIAN

THE COTTON CANDY HAND-ME-DOWN sorry excuse for an outfit that I had the misfortune to be wearing tore as I yanked the disk out of my pocket. Crouching, I placed NickNick's stolen car onto the hot black pavement. The rays of the two risen suns blazed off its silver surface like blinding arrows. "I remember, that little switch in the middle makes it grow to full size."

Gneeecey galloped up behind me, huffing and puffing. "Yeah, Ig. It's that lousy red button there. Jus' push."

Jaw clenched, I pressed it. We leaped backward as instantly, the saucer expanded to the size of a compact vehicle. Couldn't help but notice the cracked and surprisingly untinted windshield. Evidently, my lookalike liked to be seen.

Gneeecey strode up to a tire and kicked it. "Sure hope they replaced the winter air in these babies wit' summer air. Y'know, to opooptimize performance. We're stinkin' gonna need all the help we can get."

I glanced over my shoulder. "C'mon, Diroctor, help me out here. We've gotta hurry. Now, how do we freakin' get into this thing again?"

"Here, Ig." Gneeecey pushed an almost invisible indentation, and both sides flipped up.

We scrambled inside. "Now," I thought aloud, head spinning in all directions to check whether anyone was closing in on us yet, "how do we shut 'em so we can get outta here?" By chance, I hit a blinking green light on the dash. The doors slammed, and the engine roared to life.

"Good job," remarked Gneeecey. "Especially for an Ig."

"Uh, thanks."

"Y'know what they say, Ig. When one door opoopens, another one slams shut."

"Uh-huh…yeah, Diroctor. Now we've gotta figure out how to drive this freakin' thing! Quick! Before *we* get slammed! I'm trying to remember what they did."

"This thing ain't that sophistiphoosticated. It was built for lazy people. How stinkin' difooficult can it be? Ya gotta *think* like an Eccchsian!"

In the not-too-far distance, sirens blared. "Oh crap! They know we've escaped!"

Gneeecey and I began smacking icons, any and all lit on the dashboard. Windows opened and closed. Windshield wipers flapped hysterically, and a silly soprano horn started beeping nonstop. With the push of an orange arrow that pointed upward, the car grew as tall as a two-story building, one that hopped around like a pogo stick.

I felt seasick. "Diroctor, press the blue 'down' arrow there!"

He punched it. The vehicle returned to regular size and stopped springing up and down.

"We'd better be more careful," I warned. "We'd sure hate for this thing to shrink back to pocket size, with *us* stuck inside!"

"Ya got that right! That would stinkin' *stink*!"

The sirens shrieked louder.

I grasped a long rod near the center console. "Remember this?"

"Yeah, Ig, now I rememboober, that's how they made it go."

Nodding, I pulled the wiry stick back. The vehicle turned on its base three times, then began to roll forward. Recalling what Jerko had done, I tugged on a second, smaller lever and we lifted up slightly. "Okay, we're in business."

"Good work, Ig, almost as good as *I* coulda done."

"Uh…thanks," I replied, wiping perspiration from my brow as we gained speed. "Now, where are we going?"

"Away from them polices that's chasin' us!"

"You're actually right, Diroctor. We'll decide where to go *after* we freakin' get away."

"What's *this*?" inquired Gneeecey, his index finger poised over what appeared to be a yellow-lit toilet-shaped symbol.

"Don't touch it!"

"Holy Saint Bogelthorpe! My seat jus' turnt into a terlit! Right under my stinkin' bimbus! A real terlit, wit' real water down there!"

"Guess this vehicle's meant for long distance trips." The tighter I grasped the main rod, the faster we traveled. "Wonder where the brakes are," I mumbled, not buying Ebegneeezer's claims that the car was collision-proof.

A rhythmic clacking ensued as Gneeecey kept playing around with the control for the commode, causing his seat to open and close beneath him every two seconds. "Think I'll jus' put it back on regoogoolar. Ain't very comfoofortabooble, gettin' my lousy bimbus splashed."

"Uh-huh," I replied, distracted. There had to be a way to stop the freakin' car.

"Water's cold, too, Ig, y'know, real, real…*what* the?"

Suddenly, a fleet of cop cars zoomed up behind us, sirens wailing, purple and green lights flashing.

"Holy crap!" I shouted, squeezing the stick as my hammering heart plummeted into the pit of my stomach. "Couldn't stop if I freakin' wanted to!"

One by one, each police vehicle overtook us, their uniformed occupants waving and grinning.

Gneeecey and I exchanged puzzled glances. "Holy stinkin' Saint Bogelthorpe!"

I gulped. "They must think…"

"…that we're *them*!" exclaimed Gneeecey, completing my sentence.

"Yeah." I waved a trembling hand and smiled back as each cruiser zipped past. "The other you and me…out on official business. Or something."

Gneeecey chuckled. "Or *somethin'* is right!"

I exhaled as the last of the lights flickered into the horizon. "That certainly buys us a little more time."

We sped along until we reached the Palabrian Sea. Its humongous wall of waves crashed before us for as far as the eye could see. "What do I do *now*? Can't stop this dang thing, and we sure don't wanna turn around."

The car made the decision for us. We shot into the ocean, wheels retracting with a great thud.

"Careful what you say," I whispered, as a gigantic silver mylar balloon bumped up against us, "Careful what you say" painted across its side in black script. Before Gneeecey's big yapper could open all the way, I reached over and managed to cover it with my left hand.

"Y'know, Ig," shouted Gneeecey, breaking free, "I think I finally figured out how to stop this here stinkin' vehickookle!"

"*No!*" I growled. "*Not now!*"

Ignoring me, he smacked a solid red octagon on the control panel...and the engine gurgled...and died. Dozens of scarlet inflatables decorated with the white-lettered word "No" smashed up against us.

I squeezed the acceleration rod and pulled in all directions...to no avail. Our lifeless vehicle rolled sideways. "We're *trapped*," I muttered. "We'll run out of *oxygen*!"

-23-

CAR TROUBLE

GNEEECEY'S TREMBLING INDEX finger hovered over the icon that had initially started the car. Eyeballs bulging, he pressed it. And smacked it. And elbowed it. Even spat on it. Each time, the engine only churned halfheartedly. We continued to drift sideways. And downward.

The good diroctor and I stared openmouthed as an iridescent whale appeared in front of our windshield. Body glowing red and blue simultaneously—a color more difficult to describe than purple—its one bowling ball of a revolving eye stared back as it swam out of view.

"These lousy audimatical cars are no good," growled Gneeecey, still poking at the useless green symbol. "Too many stinkin' things can go wrong wit' 'em. An' they *do*."

Suddenly, we lurched forward. The great whump that followed informed us that we had hit bottom. A whirlwind of sand spiraled upward, encircling our doomed vehicle.

"Heya, Ig," asked Gneeecey, not seeming to take notice of our latest and possibly final predicament, "did ya ever taste tap water soup?"

"What?"

"Tap water soup," he repeated, still fiddling with the dead button on the dash. "It's priddy tasty."

"We're gonna be tasting some real salty soup, more than we can even handle, if that freakin' crack in the windshield can't take all the pressure down here at the bottom of…"

A weird sizzling noise cut me off. Our interior lights and icons went dark.

Gneeecey punched his fists on the dash. "Well, now we ain't gotta worry 'bout that, or nuthin' else."

I had no reply. Just sat fidgeting with my hair, wondering how much time we had left before our oxygen would run out.

Gneeecey must've read my mind. "Ig, how much time do ya think we got, y'know, before we can't respoopirate no more?"

"Diroctor, I really don't know. You're the scientist."

"I'll proboobably never, *nebberd-kinnezzard*, extra-never, see my Perswayssick County again, or my belovooved Planet Eccchs." He sniffled and blew his loud honking schnozz in the crook of his arm.

Looking away, I prayed that we wouldn't be slammed into by some gigantic underwater blimp bearing the word "Honk!"

"An' I'll never ever see my mom or dad again, poor Fritzl an' Froop, they'll sure miss me. An' my Uncle Zoology. An' my Aunt ReeUmpa, y'know, the one I tol' ya 'bout who knits them priddy plaid couches?"

"You know, Diroctor, *I've* got family too, and I'll probably never, ever see *them*…"

"An' I'll miss my F-Day that I planned so good," he continued, not even hearing me. "Me an' my fifteen million stranded snitizens will never get to flush ourselves back to our home planet! *Waaaaah!*"

We were probably too deep down to even be bumped by balloons. Shuddering, I watched an inky squid-like creature glide through the cloud of sediment that still swirled around us as a foot-high glittering gold starfish attached itself to our window.

Gneeecey's big noggin swiveled my way. "Ya lousy Ig, every stinkin' time I have anythin' to do wit'cha, it always ends up bein' some kinda disastrophy."

I bolted upright in my seat. "*What?* It was *you* who…" My voice trailed off. Wasn't worth it to waste whatever stale air might be left.

Gneeecey bowed his head. "Don't matter anyways, Ig. Now me an' you are here together in this predikookamental predikookament."

"Yep."

"Why're ya lookin' at me like that, ya lousy Ig?"

"Uh…uh…was I?" It was becoming harder to breathe, and temperatures were rising. Sweltering, I cursed NickNick's plastic bag of a polyester outfit. "Diroctor, maybe we shouldn't talk too much. We'll use up our oxygen faster."

We just sat and watched murky shadows of unearthly sea life float past. That stubborn sparkly starfish remained attached to our windshield. Closer inspection revealed its shiny body to be comprised entirely of tiny staring golden eyeballs.

"Heya, Ig, y'know what?"

My aching head turned slowly in his direction. "No. What?"

"I kinda wish this vehickookle had stalled out wit' that, y'know, terlit under my seat *open*."

-24-

WHAT WOULD THE ANSWER BEAGLE DO?

THE TWO OF US STARED through the cracked windshield of our sunken vehicle. Gneeecey broke the silence. "Y'know what, Ig?" I sighed. "No. What?" He glanced my way. "In school, Ig, we learnt 'bout our planet's legendary all-knowin' Answer Beagle. Never met the guy personally, but they assured us that he stinkin' knows everythin'. Jus' as his name impooplicates. Wonder what he would do now?"

I shrugged.

"An' y'know what else?"

"No. What else?"

He raised his sneakered right foot and pried open the front of its rubber sole. "See, Ig? It's the secret hidin' place created that time ya busted my shoe when ya creepily made your kitchen get all cleaned up all by itself. That flyin' Gobblesnotts rat was unlousy enough to bring back my treasures. The other night. Musta been him. Slipped 'em through the prison bars. While you were busy sleepin', I got the courage to look. Y'know, rememboober, we heard that noise?"

I blinked.

"Mayboobee I shouldn't call him a flyin' rat no more."

Gneeecey yanked a limper-than-limp Yammicles out of the tip of his high top, along with his thousand-dollar bill. He waved the latter in my face.

My eyes widened.

"Since I used your, uh, *resources*, y'know, wit'out securin' your actual Ig authorization when I purchoochased my beaudiful new car, I'll stinkin' *give* ya this if we make it outta here alive."

"Wonder what the odds of *that* are," I muttered. "You must think we're doomed."

"Rememboober, Ig, I learnt in my News Guessin' classes that everythin' in life is fifty-fifty. Either somethin'll hapoopen or it won't. All boils down to proboobability."

A fifty-fifty chance seemed optimistic at best.

Gneeecey pulled a gleaming object out of his sneaker and placed it in my palm. "An' here, Ig. That Mister Gobblesnotts brung this to me, too."

"My missing earring!"

He grinned. "An' y'know what else, Ig?"

I shook my head. "No...what else?"

"I'm kinda gettin' used to havin' ten fingers. Ain't *that* bad."

"I'm glad it's getting better for you."

"An' y'know what else?"

"No. What?"

"I was thinkin', if we do make it outta here, y'know, not dead, I should proboobably try an' be nicer to Flubbubb."

Couldn't argue with that.

"I mean," continued Gneeecey, "I always make such a big stinkin' stink 'bout not lettin' him play even one single lousy note on his triangle when me an' Flea do them recitals at the Perswayssick Civic Center."

I cringed, recalling the out-of-tune tooth-shattering shrieks that exploded from Gneeecey's electric violin, (or "voaline," as he so lovingly called it), and pianist Sooperflea's constant tendency to play ahead of the music because his ESP made him anticipate notes and passages way too far in advance. Perhaps Flubbubb was better off not being allowed to play. I yawned, most likely from lack of oxygen as fragments of that recurring dream featuring Flea wafted through that foggy space between my ears. Could only see his face and hear him uttering an indecipherable something. Sounded like squirm bowl. Or berm hole. Or maybe germ mole.

"Perhaphoops," said Gneeecey, also gulping for air, "I should treat Flubbubb more nicer, even though he is a real Iggleheimer."

Ah yes, those mythical, clumsy three-legged troglodytes from Gneeecey's native Planet Eccchs. A real insult to be called one...my lovely nickname 'Ig' was short for *that*.

"Although," Gneeecey added, "it might be good I don't let him play 'cause silence between notes is, y'know, very importootant. Music wouldn't be music wit'out no silent spaces between notes, right? It would all pour into your ears like bad smellin' molasses wit' no rhythm."

"Uh, well..."

"Guess I ain't been *that* rotten to Flubbubb after all."

The good diroctor might not have been blessed with musical talent, but he sure did have a gift when it came to rationalization.

"Heya, Ig..."

"What now?"

"Well, ya don't hafta answer so oogdimonious."

"Look, Diroctor, we may only have hours or even just minutes left."

"Me an' you been through lots together, ain't we, Ig?" I was surprised to see his oval peepers welled up with tears. They glistened in the dark.

"Yep. We sure have."

Nodding, he wiped his wet face on his forearm.

"So," I continued, "you think maybe, in what are possibly our last moments, you could call me by my proper name?"

"Your propooper name?"

"Yes. You know, *Nicki*."

"That ain't my name. An' y'know what else, Ig?"

It had become downright steamy in our car-turned-submarine. "What else?"

"I really kinda don't hate you."

"I really kinda don't hate you either, too."

"Another thing, Ig…"

"What?"

"Ya think them Goya beans got anything to do wit' your, y'know, havin' them special powers?"

I managed a smile. "Well, you never know."

"I was thinkin', Ig, if we ever get outta this, the nex' time I visit your dimension, mayboobee ya could gimme some, an'…"

That moment, we were bombarded by blinding blue and green beams. I shielded my eyes.

"Ig! *Looky*! Look at all them lights! Mus' be some gigaaantical killer monster!"

We soon found ourselves enveloped in the strange luminosity.

"*Wowzickles!*" yelled Gneeecey. "I wonder if this is how Fleaglossity feels, y'know, stuck in your lousy closet wit' all them weird lights!"

The brilliant hues blazed through my tightly closed lids. "Yes, poor Flea. Nice that you're developing some empathy in these last moments, Diroctor."

"Speakin' of empoopathy, Fleaglossity was inventin' some stooopid Empoopathy 5000 machine that's supposed to help him feel the pain his chiropractor patients are feelin'. So he could help 'em better. Mayboobee *that* messed him up. Who wants to feel someone else's lousy backache? Dopey idea."

"That's not dopey at all. Now, *what* is freakin' going on here?"

"Could be the Answer Beagle, Ig, here to save us! Nah—he's proboobably too busy an' importootant! Betcha it's Sooperflea! Has to be Fleaglossity, finally comin' to save us! An' look, he brung along all them lights from your closet! Yayyysickles! We're over *here*, Flea! Me an' the Ig! Good ol' Fleaglossity! We're stuck down here wit' no air in this lousy, horribooble vehickookle an'…"

A loud thump interrupted him. After a violent jerk forward, we found ourselves being towed by the eerie lights.

"What in Bogelthorpe's name's hapoopenin', Ig?"

"Dunno!" Our bodies slammed back into our seats as we picked up speed and flew through the ocean, seeing only sediment and bubbles for miles.

Gneeecey grabbed my hand. "Guess Flea knows what he's doin'! Sometimes he don't! We might possiboobly be travoovelin' at the speed of light!"

Sheer fear causing me to shiver, I squeezed his furry fingers as our wheels descended with a bang and we sped onto bumpy dry land.

In a split second, our car clunked up against whatever was dragging it, darn near giving me whiplash when we screeched to a sudden stop.

Gneeecey groaned. "Ow, my stinkin' neck! Fleaglossity always was kinda incompoopetent. Jus' managed to graduate from superhero school by the teeth of his skin." We could finally see the vehicle that had pulled us to safety. *Sea Police* painted in white lettering across it, the whale-sized amphibious aquamarine tank sported six-foot high heavy-treaded retractable tires. An array of wings, fins, periscopes, and strange cannon-like protrusions covered the conveyance. Its blinding green and purple lights continued to flash.

A muscle-bound officer, attired in a navy uniform, lumbered our way, service revolver drawn. He unlatched our doors and offered me a hand as I staggered onto the blacktop.

"*You* ain't Flea," observed an astute Gneeecey. "You ain't Fleaglossity at all! *Or* the Answer Beagle!"

"Your Grate Royal Hynesty and his assistant," he began, saluting Gneeecey, who, and I'll give him props here, had the presence of mind to reach into his endless pit of a T-shirt pocket and don a pair of sunglasses, plus clench his right fist to hide his single-index-fingered mitt.

"You both alright?" asked the officer.

"I...I think so," I replied, rubbery legs ready to collapse. "How...did you find us?"

"The ooglometronical signal emitted by your vehicle led us to you. You're much too important not to be monitored when you leave the main quadrant."

Gneeecey's face lit up.

The man stepped back. "I'm Lieutenant Krumplotsky. Special forces unit is on alert back in the hydro car. I'll inform them it's not an XL3 photon-plus cannon situation. Your vehicle was reported stolen. Possible carjacking. Or assassination attempt."

Gneeecey flinched.

The officer replaced his weapon in its holster. "Glad to recover you both unharmed."

"Yupperooney," replied Gneeecey, putting on a very poor British accent, "we are *them*."

I shot the good diroctor a withering glance. Within minutes, we could expect an APB alert to be put out for two lookalike ZomSect3 escapees.

"*She* took a wrong turn," continued Gneeecey, jutting his grimy chin in my direction. "Wasn't payin' detention. Coulda got us seriously kilt."

I bit my tongue hard. Almost tasted blood.

Lieutenant Krumplotsky pulled a translucent device, more gaseous than solid, from his belt and scrolled down its smoky screen. "According to your itinerary for today, your Grate Royal Hynesty, you're en route to the Splattsburgh Quadrant, where you're scheduled to be sworn in at 0-1200 zoggblatz for your second term."

"I'm *real* good at swearin'," replied the good dirootor.

Chuckling, the officer removed his helmet, scratched his shiny bald head and handed Gneeecey a legal-sized yellow sheet of paper. "I'm sure you are, your Grate Royal Hynesty. Here's another copy of your speech, for your convenience."

"How *very* cornvenient." Gneeecey crumpled it up and crammed it into his lumpy T-shirt pocket. "I'll keep it safe in here wit' all my other junk."

"I'll contact your limo driver immediately, Your Grate Royal Hynesty." The lieutenant tapped his tablet. "You're safe now, thanks to that UPZx3 signal tracking. If you remember, you enacted the regulation requiring that feature yourself, for both your car and hers."

Gneeecey puffed his chest out. "I bloody do rememboober. Leave it to good ol' me!"

"And no worries, we'll have your vehicle here towed back to headquarters and see if it can be salvaged. And Ms. NickNick, please be more careful next time you're transporting such precious cargo."

Gneeecey grinned. I did too, through gritted teeth.

Seconds later, a black armored limousine zoomed up alongside us.

"Jolly good job, Plotchcrum!" shouted Gneeecey, waving as the officer strode back to his hydro car, thankfully too far out of range to hear him. "Ya sure know your onions, ol' chap!"

I yanked Gneeecey by his arm. "C'mon, Diroctor, let's get in and figure out what's next. We are not out of the woods, by any means."

"We weren't *in* no woods, ya Ig. We were at the bottom of the sea. Sheesh. Where did you learn *your* geographoophy?"

I rolled my eyes as we piled into the backseat. "Mister ZeeBee!" exclaimed Gneeecey, greeting the familiar zebra-humanoid who had driven us into town back when we'd first arrived.

"Your Grate Royal Hynesty, my stroke of good fortune is *three-fold!* I am now employed by you an' your wonderful government, an' encouraged by your promise today at breakfast to reconsider the release of my twin brother from ZomSect3 for good behavior. An' I am simply delighted to be transportin' you an' your lovely companion *twice* today!"

"I'm simpooply delighted too, Mister ZeeBee, but if ya rekookolect, as I informed ya las' time, she ain't my companion. An' she certaintaneously ain't lovooverly. She's jus' my stinkin' assistant, the Ig."

"In your freakin' dreams," I muttered.

"Sorry, Your Grate Royal Hynesty," replied the zebra-humanoid, brushing his unruly red mane from his eyes. "You seemed to appreciate her much more this mornin' when you hired me. An' Miss NickNick, I'll never forget your kind words either."

Squirming, I forced a smile.

"W-we are g-goin' to the…uh…Splattsburgh Quadrant," stuttered Gneeecey, unwittingly dropping his English accent. "Gotta get sweared in an' make a real important pollutical speech. So, let's step on it. Don't wanna miss my own inordination."

"Your Grate Royal Hynesty, it is my mission to deliver you in a timely fashion."

"Okie-doke, ol' bloke," replied Gneeecey, once again attempting to sound British.

"Your Grate Royal Hynesty," said Mister ZeeBee, eyeing us in his rearview mirror, "I realize that I'm to drive you directly to your destination, but perhaps, before the police escort meets up with us in New Dwonksville, we should swing by your mansion so that the two of you could…uh…no offense intended…freshen up a bit?"

Gneeecey and I exchanged glances. He straightened his shirt and wiped his runny nose on the edge of his short sleeve, no easy feat. I smoothed down my cyclone-styled hair. We must've looked a real sight.

"I know a shortcut," insisted the striped chauffeur. "I'd be happy to wait."

"No!" Gneeecey and I shouted, in unison.

"No, *thanks!*" I added, for emphasis, in a voice as tight and squeaky as Gneeecey's.

-25-

ANTIDISESTABLISHMENTARIANISTICALLY
SPEAKIN'

AS SOON AS SIGNS for New Dwonksville city limits popped up, an army of police cars and motorcycles roared up alongside our limo. Beaming, Mister ZeeBee gave our escorts a vigorous thumbs up signal.

"*Wowzickles!*" Gneeecey leaned forward. "Looky, Ig! I mus' be priddy stinkin' importootant!"

I nudged him. He took no notice. Mouth agape, his head turned in all directions. I sighed. "Looky at all them polices!" he squealed. "Gonna suggesticate this kinda security for *meee* at our nex' Quality of Life Commission meetin', *if* I ever stinkin' get home, that is."

"You will most *certainly* get home, Your Grate Royal Hynesty," our driver assured him. "After your inauguration an' gala celebration at the Virgil Vomker Pavilion, you, your beaudiful wife, an' your two daughters will return home together. You got my personal guarantee."

"Hah?"

"Your family's already at the pavilion, Your Grate Royal Hynesty, awaitin' your triumphant arrival. An' I must say, you certainly have a lovely family."

Gneeecey's schnozz crinkled. "Yeah. Lovooverly."

We could see Mister ZeeBee's smiling face reflected in his rearview mirror. "Girls sure are gettin' big."

Before Gneeecey could open his mouth, a deep voice came crackling over the vehicle's police scanner. "Prisoner breakout at ZomSect3. Situation fluid, will advise as additional info becomes available."

Mister ZeeBee's stripes appeared to vanish as the blood drained from his face. Adrenaline shot through my veins and Gneeecey began to chew on his left wrist, setting off the alarm on his watch.

✳ ✳ ✳

"IN HERE NOW!" barked a tall bodyguard.

Tunnels terrified me. I just stood in place, body rigid.

He yanked me by the arm, nearly dislocating my shoulder as he pulled me in. "I said, *now!*"

"Not very befittin' of someone of my stinkin' standin'," complained Gneeecey as dozens of shadowy figures rushed him through the pitch-black passageway.

I stumbled along behind them.

"Don't smell too good in here, neitherwise," Gneeecey added, forgetting to fake his English accent.

"Your Grate Royal Hynesty," began a gruff voice, "there's been a breakout in ZomSect3. Some key prisoners are missing. Can't take any chances."

"Stinkin' whaaatevah," answered the good diroctor in what sounded like a Southern drawl. "We'll be sure to disgust this all later, after mah upchuckin' inordination."

"Yes, Your Grate Royal Hynesty."

After what seemed like a half-hour of being jostled around in total darkness, a blinding light greeted us. Gneeecey slapped his shades back on.

"Ten steps here lead right up to the dais," said a guard. "Plan remains the same. Make your speech, you're sworn in, then we whisk you away to the festivities."

Gneeecey dug his right hand into his pocket. "Righto, jolly ol' daft chap."

"Your Igglet will sit here," said the tall one, speaking about me as if I weren't even there. He escorted me to a folding metal chair adjacent to the lectern. "Anyone seen Jerko? Sure could use an extra body here."

"Um...uh...I think he's wit' the...uh...wife an' kids," replied Gneeecey, trying his best to sound casual.

Squinting, I shifted in my hard seat and looked out upon the massive crowd of humans and canine-humanoids that overflowed from the grandstand right up to the edge of the security-lined stage. I spied Brad and Meg. And Clyde. And Vlatta and Velma. They stood out in the open, practically right on top of the guards, glaring up at us, faces hardened with defiance. All except for the glazy-eyed zebra-humanoid, who just gazed into space. So much for escaped prisoners and all that security.

Confident that my hair actually did resemble a living tornado, I attempted again to flatten it with both palms.

Gneeecey strode up to the microphone, sunglasses perched precariously across his twitching snout. With a grand flourish, he ripped his speech out of his shirt pocket, tearing it in half.

He cleared his throat. "Fiends, country peepooples an' fine snitizens of this wonderfooful land of HyenaZitania, we are assemboobled here for a very momentical occasion, where I will make my pollutical speech an' tell youse all what I am gonna accompooplish in my nex' term."

Thunderous cheers erupted, except from the escapees up front, whose jaws and fists remained clenched.

"Eh—who stinkin' needs *this*?" Energized by the crazed crowd, Gneeecey tossed his torn speech onto the wooden planks below. "I awready read it. Once. Got me one of them photootographical memories. I will talk directly to youse, my jolly peepooples! Tally-ho!"

My heart sank. Gneeecey was sure to mess up now.

"First," he shouted, his British accent evaporating, "youse are all lucky youse live here, where most stuff is not only legal, it's illegal too!"

He hadn't taken his meds for days. I cradled my pounding head in my hands.

"An' wit'out getting' sentimentrental," he continued, "I pledge to stinkronize our moolitary might wit' everythin' I can do to make yooou, my wonderfooful snitizens, hapoopy! I will still give you the shirts offa your backs! An' the pants offa your bimbus, too!"

More deafening applause. The two suns fried my neck as they blazed through an opening in the canopy above. Melting inside my polyester puke-pink and sickly green plastic bag of an outfit, feeling faint, I cursed my misfortune.

"Yolo, baby!" shrieked Gneeecey. "Youse only live once! An' we are certaintaneously gonna live that once, *twice*!"

Frenzied onlookers threw hats and water bottles up into the blue sky, the killer rays of the suns ricocheting like lightning bolts from the clear containers.

Gneeecey pumped both fists into the air. "An' ya know what else? I've fixed it so youse can plug appliances an' all other 'lectrical stuff into every tree trunk in this fair land! They're all grounded now, wit' them three-pronged adapters! Even the ones on Gruntt Avenue, y'know, where we had sevooveral dangerousical incidents! An' now they all got USB ports, too! The *trees*, not the incidents!"

Onlookers clapped and stomped.

Evidently, Gneeecey had glanced at his speech before tossing it. Sort of.

"An' now we're addin' yellow to them lousy blue laws to get green laws!"

He was making up stuff now.

"An' why," he asked, remembering again to speak like a Brit, "should we be allowed to buy vanilla syrup every stinkin' day, but chokookolate syrup only on some days? That could stinkin' cause anarkooky! Even among *meee*!"

"We want chocolate!" chanted the crowd. "We want chocolate!"

"An' antidisestablishmentarianistically speakin'," he continued, "concernin' my metaphorical rise to power, I'm hapoopy to serve once more, wit' all due disrespect, as your Grate Kiss Butt, an' I thereforthically pledge..."

A collective gasp, mine included, interrupted his declaration. He had gotten his title wrong.

"An' yeah-an'-a-half," he added, realizing his blunder, "I mayboobee mighta changed my title slightly, to conserve vowels an' consonants, in order to bring more eckookoonomical an' alphoophabetical equality an' justice to this fair land! It's a new stinkin' day!"

The cheering resumed. Surprisingly, security seemed to take no notice of the good dirroctor's speech and character discrepancies. They just stood around staring vacantly, except when they peered down at their wristwatches (which was often).

Gneeecey bowed in every direction, so deeply, that the back seam of his trousers split. No one seemed to notice. Except for me. And the escaped prisoners up front, plus that six-foot-tall teal alligator in a chrome yellow plaid zoot suit. They all snickered with glee.

A spindly old human whose severe facial features appeared to have been chiseled by a furious sculptor, shuffled up to the hissing microphone. Holding out a thick poop-brown tome, he addressed Gneeecey, in a nasal tone. "Your Grate Royal Hynesty, please step forward and place your right hand on our revered plookenblook."

Gneeecey obliged, revealing a right hand that featured only a single index finger. Thankfully, it seemed to go unnoticed.

"Repeat after me," said the humorless man, as the skies above suddenly became overcast, "I, Ebegneeezer Gesundheit Eeeceygnay, swear to uphold the laws of our great, double-sunned planet of HyenaZitania, and faithfully serve a thirteenth term as Grate BiggButtKizz…"

"Imposter!" howled Ebegneeezer as he sprinted onstage from the back entrance, flanked by Jerko, NickNick, and swarms of black-suited bodyguards, too many to count, weapons drawn.

-26-

WE AIN'T *THEM*

THE LECTERN OVERTURNED as I grabbed Gneeecey by the neck of his T-shirt. Through a thickening white haze, I could just about see that we stood face-to-face with Ebegneeezer, Jerko and NickNick. My double's razor-sharp crimson fingernails were aimed at my face, no doubt ready to scratch out my eyeballs.

"Don't jus' stinkin' *staaand* there! *Dooooo* somethin'! Ig! *Pleeeease!*" screamed Gneeecey.

Didn't even stop to consider in that split second that Gneeecey had actually uttered the word "please." I just about heard him as the jet engines in my skull began to rumble. My narrowed eyes remained focused on our three adversaries and the mob of bodyguards bearing down upon us.

In an instant, they all froze, in mid-leap.

"Ig, ya *done* it!"

"C'mon, let's go! They're not gonna stay like this forever!"

The stage trembled beneath our feet as the crowd rushed onto it, determined to get up close to the guy who gave them the shirts off their backs. Gneeecey and I took off, weaving our way through bodies in motion like football players.

Arms outstretched, our friends, the undetected escapees, helped us down.

"We ain't *them*!" shouted the good diroctor, flopping into Brad Shipman's hands.

Brad set Gneeecey down. "We know. Remember *us*, your buddies from ZomSect3?"

Clyde motioned to us. "Yeah, fancy meeting *you* here. Okay, follow me!"

Our swift exit went unnoticed as the dark-suited thugs, who had come back to life, and outnumbered security scrambled all over, engaged in a losing battle. I spotted Mister ZeeBee's brother. Spooked, his wild red mane flew as he galloped out of sight on all fours.

Meanwhile, we managed to squeeze through a surprising gap in a chain link fence and hightail it out of there, off the pavilion grounds and into the adjacent forest. Walls of towering prickly bushes, maybe ten feet tall, provided cover but ripped at our flesh and drew blood.

Gneeecey's long sneakered feet became tangled in vines and roots and other detritus. "Which way we goin'? It's priddy stinkin' dark in here! Gotta siddown!"

"Yeah," agreed Brad. "Let's stop for a moment and get our bearings. Can't really tell which way we're going."

The emerald canopy of leaves above us all but obliterated any daylight. "Not having much luck with my GPS app here," said Clyde, chuckling halfheartedly as he swiped away on his device. "At least *they* can't find us if *we* can't find us."

Deep in thought, I lowered myself onto a petrified log, certainly feeling no sympathy for Ebegneeezer, but acknowledging that it must've been traumatic for his daughters to witness that whole onstage debacle...I wondered what was happening there now…cops had to be searching for us.

Muttering something about hating everyone and everything, especially trees and bushes, Gneeecey flumped down in front of me.

"Let us take this opportunity to ponder whether we're heading east or west," proposed Velma.

"And that promises to be quite a test," added Vlatta. Leaves crackled as she and her sister plopped themselves down onto the ground.

Clyde sighed. "Not getting *any* kind of signal out here."

The seven of us sat in silence, mood as gloomy as our surroundings.

"We'll be okay," said Brad, after a couple minutes. "I believe that justice and good always prevail."

"Me too," replied Clyde, nodding. "That's what keeps us going."

"Well, stinkin' justice better hurry up," said Gneeecey. "My pants are busted an' these lousy plaaants here are makin' my bimbus itch. Sure hope they ain't poisonous ivy! Had that once, couldn't sit for weeks!" He jumped up and began scratching vigorously.

"Look!" cried Meg, pointing upward. "Suns are out again!"

Brad peered up. A brilliant shaft of light angled through an aperture in the dark forest ceiling. "Now we've got some sense of direction. We know which way to head now, and we can…"

An ear-splitting clap of thunder interrupted him.

"How can *that* be, if the suns are out?" asked Meg.

Clyde rose. "Have no idea. Let's get outta here. Not good to be under trees during electrical storms."

"Yeah, real dangerousical. Trees don't even look like they're grounded," agreed Gneeecey. "Ain't seen no outlets or USB ports on *any* of 'em. They jus' look like regoogoolar trees."

"Let's just follow that glow," said Velma, helping her sister up.

Vlatta brushed off her posterior. "I'm in absolute agreement, you know."

We staggered toward the sunbeams.

"Can't keep up wit' youse peopoople," groused Gneeecey. "An' I sure stinkin' hope there ain't no agoogilators or crockookadiles in here to get me!"

Laughing, Clyde pivoted and scooped the good diroctor up onto his shoulders. "I'll carry anyone who's fighting against the tyranny!"

"Yes," agreed Meg, slogging alongside me. "You two helped us. Now it's our turn to help you."

After stumbling around for what seemed like a half hour, we reached a clearing.

"We can take cover behind there," suggested Clyde, his eyes fixed on an elongated gray single-story building.

Brad adjusted his soaked white T-shirt. "Sounds like a plan."

"Yep," agreed Meg, perspiration plastering her blond bangs to her forehead. "Only plan around."

Gneeecey, still traveling atop Clyde's shoulders, remained uncharacteristically quiet as we sprinted down the blacktop. Huffing and puffing, I glanced over at the elderly sisters, shocked that they were able to keep up, not even breaking a sweat as they flew down the road in their tight pinstriped skirts. They put me to shame. Decades younger, I was ready to drop.

When we finally reached the warehouse, I leaned back against a rough cinder block wall, gasping for air.

Velma's kind baby blues flashed my way. "With time, you'll learn to develop and control your considerable powers."

"And," added Vlatta, smiling, "you'll gain wisdom like ours."

Before I could respond, a jagged lightning bolt shattered the postcard blue skies.

We gawked as a multicolored holographic test pattern materialized above our heads. Comprised of translucent horizontal stripes, it stretched and curved from where we stood all the way to a point in the far distance.

"*This way*," boinged a familiar voice that seemed to emanate from the unearthly rainbow.

"*Flea-glos-sity!*" Gneeecey shrieked, smacking the top of Clyde's head with each syllable. "Sounds jus' like *Flea!*"

"*This way!*" pleaded the voice again. "*Take the wormhole!*"

"*Gotta* be stinkin' Flea!"

My eyes widened in a storm of discovery. That's what Flea had been trying to tell me, in those weird dreams. *Wormhole!*

"Let's see where that strange light ends," suggested Clyde, repositioning Gneeecey on his shoulders. "An' uh, Diroctor or whatever your name is, if you pound on my head one more time, you're on your own. I'll put'cha right down and leave ya here."

Gneeecey's yapper opened, but no words escaped as we continued our mad dash.

We ran forever but didn't seem to be making progress. We weren't any closer to the light. Didn't know how much longer I could keep going. The asphalt felt harder with each step, giving my sore knees a real pounding. The unrelenting suns showed no mercy either, and there wasn't a tree in sight, metallic or otherwise.

In an instant, the kaleidoscopic arch above shifted, accompanied by a deafening thunderclap that reverberated through my entire body. The design in the sky morphed, before our very eyes, into a diaphanous scarlet tunnel. It extended down to the ground, only yards away. "*Back to our universe*," echoed the goofy voice we had heard before. "*Back to our universe!*"

We all skidded to a stop.

Vlatta screamed, "*Holy…*"

"*…moly!*" shouted Velma, completing her sister's thought.

Brad's jaw dropped. Meg, equally lost for words, grabbed his arm and gazed ahead.

"A wormhole of some kind," marveled a wide-eyed Clyde.

"Looky, Ig! Flea musta broke outta your lousy closet!"

Despite the heat, I found myself shivering. "*Holy crap!*"

Then sirens began wailing.

Clyde lowered Gneeecey onto the sidewalk and turned to me. "You two take that wormhole. Should hopefully get you back home. At any rate, it'll get you outta *here!*"

"We'd better get outta here too," said Brad, glancing over his shoulder.

Meg nodded. "We'd better scatter."

"No worries, guys, got our ride right here," replied Clyde, winking as he pulled a silver disk out of his pocket and plunked it onto the pavement. He pressed the enlarger switch, and we all sprang backward as it expanded to full size. "Okay, squeeze in. Just enough space for us five. Now, let's get outta here! An' good luck, you two. Just enter that wormhole, and with luck, you should be home free!"

Lips twitching, I managed a smile. "Thank you so much…for *everything!*"

After they all piled in and the doors slammed shut, Clyde's window slid open. "You'd better take advantage of that wormhole—like *now!* Those suckers have been known to disappear, just like *that!*" He snapped his fingers. "Ciao!"

The vehicle sped off, reflecting the tangerine hues of the setting suns.

"C'mon, Diroctor!" I grabbed Gneeecey's hand. "You heard what he said!"

"*Nicki! Zig!*" bellowed the voice in the sky. "*Hurry!*"

I dragged Gneeecey forward. "C'mon! You hear those sirens?"

"Wait, Ig! Yammicles fell outta my shoe! Back *there*!" He broke free from my grip and sprinted several yards back, toward a limp brown heap laying on the sidewalk. "An' *looky*, here's my thousan'-dollar bill!"

As he gathered up his belongings, more thunder cracked overhead. Two seconds later, the entire tunnel dematerialized. The unearthly colored lights in the sky flickered out. Totally disappeared.

I dropped to my knees. "The *wormhole*," I sobbed, wringing my hands in despair, "it's *gone*! Now we'll *never* get home!"

-27-

THE CLAW MACHINE

BLOOD FROM MY SCRAPED KNEES trickled down my shins as I pushed up off the pavement. Oblivious, Gneeecey darted past me and tore toward a humongous claw machine that had suddenly appeared in the middle of the road, from out of nowhere.

"*Holy Saint Bogelthorpe!*" he whooped. "Looky at all them cool *threes* an' *eights!*"

I ran after him. "Diroctor, *no!* It's a *trick!* They had to be listening in! Remember that night back in the dungeon when you were talking about…"

"Don't wanna hear it, ya lousy Ig!" Wet nose pressed up against the glass case, he yanked on the giant lever that manipulated the steel pincer. "Gonna get me summa them there beaudiful threes! An' faboobulous eights—they're *double* threes!"

"No, Diroctor! *Please!*"

"Aaaah…these lousy claws don't never work…it's a rip off! Machines are rigged! Well, jus' watch me! I'm gonna *beat* the stinkin' system!"

Meanwhile, sirens wailed and tires screeched all around us. "Oh crap! Diroctor, *c'mon*—we've gotta get outta here! *Now!*"

No reaction. Whatsoever.

"*Diroctor Gneeecey!*" I yelled.

"Jus' looky at all them priddy sparkly threes an' eights! Don't even gotta put no *mon-ney* in this stooopid machine! Ain't even got no *slot!* It's all stinkin' *free* for the takin'!" He took a leap, appearing to defy gravity as he and his squeaky sneakers scrambled up the side panel. Once on top, he lifted a handle. "*Looky! It opens!*"

My jaw dropped. In an instant, Gneeecey was inside the machine, sitting waist-deep in a pile of sparkly numbers of every color and material imaginable. Red, blue, green, silver, gold... plastic, rubber, metal, wood, mylar, velour and more.

My fingers flew everywhere in search of a way to open the dang thing and get him out. I groaned when I realized that the top latch had locked.

Time stood still as Gneeecey tossed numerals all over the place, his face aglow with rapture. "Orange threes! Purpoople eights! All *mine!*"

I pummeled the window with both fists. "You come out of there right now! I thought you were smarter than this! It's a *trick!*"

"This mus' be stinkin' *heaven!*" he continued, as he rubbed an inflatable yellow three under his arms and all over his torso, like the soap he never used. "If I gotta be stranded in a difooferent universe, mayboobee it really ain't gonna be so baaad!"

Footsteps and shouts were getting louder by the second.

My heart began banging through my ribcage. "Diroctor! Out! *Now!* They're gonna take us back to prison—or *worse!*"

Laughing, the crazed canine-humanoid started stuffing threes and eights into his pockets until they tumbled out. "Pockookets ain't big 'nuff! What am I gonna *dooo?*"

"Just where I knew they'd be!" shouted Ebegneeezer, scampering toward us. NickNick followed, right on his gleaming leather heels, her sword-like burgundy claws bared.

Jerko appeared, brandishing a brown pistol so tiny, it would've looked silly under other circumstances. "Haah, haah, haah, my plan worked! I should get a raise. But I'm sure I won't—never *do!*"

Seething, I concentrated my gaze upon the claw machine until that white haze obscured my vision. I wasn't entirely surprised when the entire glass case shattered, spraying zillions of fragments high into the air.

As jagged shards rained down upon our heads, Gneeecey sprang out of the machine, glaring at me. "Ya lousy Ig! Looky wha'cha jus' *done!* Ya *busticated* all them precious threes an' eights! Ya stinkin' *destructified* 'em! I'll have ya *arresticated!*"

Ebegneeezer's luminous purple peeper blazed as he pressed his extra index finger against Gneeecey's running black honker. "Speaking of criminal offenses, you didn't actually, *seriously* believe that you would succeed in impersonating *me*, The Grate BigButtKizz of this wonderful planet, *did* you, old chap?"

Eyes bulging, Gneeecey waved his fists in the air. "Ya repooprimandin' *meee*, The Grate One? Ya should stinkin' pay me for improoveratin' your lousy speech, for starters! An' go kizz your ungreat big butt!"

"Oh, *really?*"

"Yeah!" shouted Gneeecey, tugging at his own grimy blue T-shirt. "An' how do ya like my lousy red shirt here that ain't really blue that I'm wearin'?"

"Why, old chap, that tasteless piece of apparel you are sporting—*and* I may add, never seem to take off or ever launder—is *turquoise*, not red!"

"Nah, it's stinkin' *red*, like your dumb parrot Ol' Blue, ya dopey, lousy imposter!"

"Your shirt *is* stinking," replied Ebegneeezer. "As is your effort to deceive me."

"Oh *yeah*?" Gneeecey lunged at his double.

"Okay, that's it." Jerko aimed his pistol at the good director's head, stopping him in his tracks.

I took a step forward and through narrowed eyelids concentrated on the gun until it liquified like chocolate left out in the summer sun. The gangster could only gawk as his weapon dripped from his pudgy hand into a dark puddle on the sidewalk.

NickNick grabbed my arm. "Now she's really gonna pay! *Finally!*"

"I got this, babe," interrupted the gangster, reaching into his jacket.

"Yeah, right." My double raised her deadly hands to my face. I caught her by her wrists before she could do damage.

"Stop! Let *go!*" she shrieked, saucer-like eyes spinning. "You're *burning* me!"

I shook her. Hard.

"Stop! You're melting my *hair!*" Indeed, her raven hair had begun to dribble down her shoulders.

"I can do more than that," I bellowed, shaking her again. "You wanna see?"

Jerko stood gaping. "Where's all them cops that came wit' us?"

"Right behind you," I replied. "Frozen like statues, in case you hadn't noticed."

"*Please,*" pleaded NickNick as she fought in vain to break loose from my iron grip, "don't hurt me! We look alike—we *are* alike! We can be *friends!*"

Tears flooded down her face, making a mess as they mixed with her truly flowing tresses. Blinking, I shoved her away.

"Please don't *kill* me!" she screamed, flying backward. "It would be like killing yourself! I'm part of *you*, you're part of *me!*"

"*Get…out…of…my…sight*," I ordered her, emphasizing each word. Didn't recognize my own voice. Couldn't even tell if it came from my mouth or my mind.

Nearly hairless, she scuttled out of sight, bawling.

"Okay, little Miss Witch," said Jerko, turning to me as he produced a streamlined silver weapon dotted with blinking yellow lights, "you ain't no match for this here high-tech ray gun."

"Don't bet on it," I muttered, muscles tensed.

He glanced around and smiled. Police backup, still motionless, resembled the ancient Chinese Terracotta Army. He turned to Ebegneeeezer. "An' *you*, Boss, tables sure are turned *now*, ain't they? Think I like bein' treated like a underpaid third-class citizen all these years? I'm *sick* of workin' for ya!"

"Jerko, old boy, let us discuss this, perhaps over a hot toddy. I have never treated you in such a manner…and planting that claw machine idea there was *mine*, as well…"

"I can get ridda you right now, tell everyone you're away on business, and they'll believe me. Even your wife will. Got it all figured out."

"That is not advisable. You shall never get away with such a devious scheme."

"Now, both of youse dogs are gonna listen to *me*." The creep turned to Gneeecey. "You, gimme that thousand-dollar bill! I know ya got it. I seen it. It's inside your busted shoe there! An' it *ain't* worthless—that's jus' another one of the boss's lies!"

Gneeecey climbed me like a tree. "Ain't givin' nobody *nuthin*'! That mon-ney's *ours*, right Ig?"

"An' Boss, I ain't done wit' *you*, by no means," Jerko growled, before I could even frame my mouth to answer.

Ebegneeezer clung to my left leg. Gneeecey, standing on my shoulders, tightened his arms around my neck and screeched, "*Threeeee fordy-twooo bluuuuue!*"

A vivid violet blaze engulfed us, then everything went pitch-black.

-28-

F-DAY

FLAT ON MY BACK in a blue-petaled flower bed, my heart sank in increments as I took it all in. "Boss, it didn't work!" yowled Altitude. "We all flushed our terlits at the right time, jus' like ya said to, but it didn't get us back to our home planet!" The giant black-and-white mouse's voice cracked as he scurried in frantic lopsided circles.

Meanwhile, Gneeecey lay stretched out on his lawn, grinning the dopiest grin this side of the universe.

A dazed Sooperflea sat nearby, on an upside-down lawn chair, his red cape tattered. Rocking back and forth, he sported Gneeecey's battered civil defense helmet. The one with the black letter "F" painted on the front. "Oh…it worked…in more ways than one," he mumbled.

"Might not be back on our Planet Eccchs, but I sure got away from that other universe," said Gneeecey. "The one wit' that lousy, rotten other meee." The good diroctor's arms and legs flailed as he made snowless snow angels in his overgrown lime, emerald, and olive plaid tartan grass. "An' this is defoonitively *my* stinkin' yard. Ain't purpoople. An' it got that good ol' funny smell, y'know, like goth poop."

I shuddered, remembering Gneeecey's vicious prehistoric-yet-futuristic razor-sharp-fanged chrome pets, Ozzy and Vizzy.

"An' Fleaglossity," continued the good dirollector as he spat the shredded remains of a health cigar at him, "gimme back my lousy civil defense hat."

"Here, Zig." The black canine-humanoid flung the headgear at Gneeecey.

"Don't 'Zig' me. An' don't throw it. I see ya bent the stinkin' propellers. Had that lousy hat specially specifoofically made."

Sooperflea sighed. "Welcome home to you, too."

Gneeecey sat up. "Well, ya don't hafta say it like that, Fleaglossity, so oogdimonious. An' who told ya to get stuck in the lousy Ig's closet? What in Bogelthorpe's name were ya doin' in her Earth dimension anyways?"

"That Empathy 5000 machine I invented malfunctioned. Y'know, the one I was buildin' to feel my chiropractic patients' pain, so's I could help 'em better? Told ya, I can't be a superhero forever. Gettin' too old. Gotta make this second career a success."

"It was proboobably your stooopid empoopathy apooparatus that landed ya stuck in that weird light in her dumb closet. Always said that concraption was a dopey idea. Who in their right stinkin' mind wants to feel someone else's pain? Sheeeeesh!"

"Wouldn't expect *you* to understand."

"All I understandicate is that ya really messed up, Fleaglossity. As usual."

"Y'know, Zig, it wasn't no picnic on my end either. I got sucked through several wormholes. *Begged* ya to take that last one. The red one. But'cha took no notice."

"Had more important stuff to pay detention to," said Gneeecey, as he yanked an inflatable gold three out of his T-shirt pocket.

"Y'mean '*attention*'."

"Stinkin' whatever, Fleaglossity. An' stop corrugatin' my lousy English."

"An' by the way, Zig, I gotta tell ya, even though my empathy machine malfunctioned, since I been usin' it, my ESP powers have started kickin' in again."

"Stinkin' whatever, Fleaglossity."

"How do ya think I knew you an' Nicki were in trouble?"

"Mayboobee 'cause we're always in trouboobole?"

The superhero chuckled. "Y'know, Zig, I *do* got somethin' to thank ya for."

Gneeecey's eyes brightened. "I stinkin' *love* bein' thanked for stuff!"

"Your F-Day, everyone flushin' their high-tech toilets at once, generated the powerful force that freed me from Nicki's closet and that prison of light. Created the wormholes, too. Thanks. I really mean it, Zig."

Hugging his shiny three, Gneeecey grinned. "You're smellcome."

Sooperflea staggered over to me. "Hey, Nicki, did ya get any of the telepathic messages I was sendin' ya? Y'know, 'bout the wormhole?"

I stared right through him. "Uh-huh."

"Ya look extra purple, my friend. Ya okay?"

"Don't think so, Flea." Moaning, I forced my achy body into a sitting position and gazed up at Gneeecey's four-story gray stone mansion. It hadn't changed since my last unwitting visit. Tears burned down my cheeks. I was stranded in Perswayssick County…*again*…and this time with worsened dimension burn.

"Yupperooney!" squealed Gneeecey. "I swear on my ten lousy fingers, we're *home*! Home, sweet stinkin' *home*!"

"Yeah," I murmured, shielding my eyes from the arrows of sunlight that shot off his castle's highly polished five zillion windows, "*you* may be home. But what about *me?*"

Gneeecey chuckled. "*Whuddabout* you?"

"Yes," chimed in Ebegneeezer, kneeling in the dirt several yards down. He wagged his extra index finger my way. "What *about* her?"

THE BIMBUS

THANKS & GET FREE INTERVIEW!

NICKI, GNEEECEY, SOOPERFLEA, and I (and the rest of the gang, bad guys included!) thank you so much for reading "You Can't Unscramble the Omelet."

I'd be ever so grateful if you'd take a moment to leave a brief review, even just a few words, on the site where you purchased this book.

Please check out my website at www.gneeecey.com for photos of the furry folks who served as inspiration for my characters, plus a short video where we invade Gneeecey's (unlocked, as usual) bathroom, and much more!

If you email Gneeecey directly at gneeecey333@gmail.com and type "Interview" in the subject line, he'll be "severely hapoopy" to send you your free transcript of the interview that he did with me on his GAS Broadcast Network. (He's convinced that the piece makes me look bad!)

Thanks again,
Vicki

ABOUT THE AUTHOR

Vicki Solá and her long-running radio program *Que Viva La Música*, heard on 89.1 WFDU-FM and streamed worldwide at wfdu.fm, provide the New York-Metro community and beyond with salsa and Latin jazz.

Featured on *American Latino TV*, she has also served as an advisor to the Smithsonian Institution. Her articles have appeared in internationally circulated trade periodicals.

As Solá established her show, she worked full-time at a New York Spanish commercial station and part-time at a faraway one that offered oldies along with fishing reports. She attended evening classes where professors apologized for keeping her up. She also performed freelance production, usually at three a.m.

In short, she spent years guzzling black coffee, gulping down cold pizza, and walking into walls.

After Solá banged her head against a particularly hard cinder block, it dawned on her that the stories she was cranking out were autobiographical. She felt compelled to share them. *You Can't Unscramble the Omelet* is the sequel to her Sci-Fi/Fantasy novel, *The Getaway That Got Away*. Both works detail the adventures of Nicki Rodriguez, (an alternate version of the author) as she meets up with zany extraterrestrial megalomaniac canine-humanoid, Gneeecey.

Solá lives in Regular New Jersey (as opposed to Gneeecey's usually undetectable New Jersey), with her son Frank.

ACKNOWLEDGMENTS

I sit here unlacing my trusty red high tops, after having gone undercover in canine humanoid Gneeecey's universe to bring you back another tail…er…uh…tale. (Earthlings blend right in when sporting these sneakers—nobody in Perswayssick County gives you a second look).

During my perilous expedition, I began to wonder, does what we write already exist in another dimension, somewhere out there, or maybe *in* there?

Gneeecey argues that the writer creates the actual reality. "Perhaphoops, youse humans make up all this dumb junk," he says. "Then *us* poor peopoople gotta stinkin' suffer through it." (He most likely prefers this explanation because it relieves him of responsibility for his actions).

As I kick off my worn sneaks and settle in front of my laptop, copious notes and dark chocolate in hand, I conclude that whether we document what already is or invent what becomes, or just make up stuff as Gneeecey claims, one thing is for sure. I must thank all who have supported my latest mission, the writing and publishing of *You Can't Unscramble the Omelet*, sequel to *The Getaway That Got Away*.

I express utmost appreciation to my brother, Salvador F. Solá, III, for his editorial skills, invaluable feedback, and championing of every effort I undertake. My hat remains off to the still disproportionately cool Jay Hudson, whose illustrations grace my book covers. A phenomenal artist, he has demonstrated an astonishing ability to create exactly what's in my head, plus some!

Marysol Cerdeira (who emboldened the already bold Gneeecey by suggesting, "Unleash your inner Gneeecey!") and José Calderón (who first introduced the canine humanoid to delectable Tap Water Soup) have given me spiritual strength, and inspiration, on so many levels. I love you both to Gneeecey's Planet Eccchs and back!

My longtime "Sister from another planet" Connie Grossman and her late mom Audrey Grossman have encouraged and energized me—totally getting it, from Day One! And special thanks to Connie's son Sam Leviatin, for getting it and for providing Gneeecey with some great, not *grate*, ideas! (Sam is also a much better violinist and all-around musician than The Grate One. Sorry, Gneeecey, even your sharps are flat).

Realization of this project was greatly aided by the generosity of longtime friends—family, really—Richie and Michele Bertrán, staunch supporters of all my endeavors these past two decades, and my amazing sister and devoted fellow animal advocate, Judy Storkamp.

I thank my dear friend Rick Rivera for his feedback, taking the time to read my manuscripts, and for getting the word out about my work. (Not only is he one of Gneeecey's confidants, but he also knows the good diroctor's plumbing store proprietor Steve Squiggleman pretty well).

To my radio listeners and cherished community, thank you from the bottom of my heart for your love and support. ¡Que Viva La Música!

Writers groups are critical (no pun intended) necessities for authors who aspire to produce their best work possible. I am deeply grateful to Barry Sheinkopf and his First Mondays, Michael Potter's For The Love of Words, Melissa Singlevich's Writers and Authors, and Angela Artemis's Pascack Valley Writers Workshop.

I offer sincere thanks to Judy DeAngelis for her encouragement and belief in me, and to Jeremy Salter and Steven Swank, who provided thoughtful critiques and marvelous insights.

Latin Beat Magazine's Rudy and Yvette Mangual, and *Descarga*'s Bruce Polin, first gave me the opportunity to write and be published. For this, I remain eternally grateful.

A most special moment for me occurred during a recent Teaneck High School reunion when I personally handed a copy of my first book to one of my favorite teachers, John Brancato. I hope, one salubrious weekend, he'll enjoy this read. Three other exceptional educators, Beulah Warshaw, Vincentine Cundari, and Marian Shelby are no longer with us, but the impact made by each upon me has been profound and lasting.

My friend, late playwright and Obie Award winner Louis Delgado's work and very life continue to inspire me to do and be my personal best.

Speaking of personal best, my late parents Salvador F. Solá, M.D. and Hedda Solá-Westhead gave me the best of themselves and are present in all that I do and am. I'm always hoping they're reading over my shoulder as I write.

Kudos to my precious son Frank S. Grillo for his continued patience as I sat typing (and talking to myself, still do) for hours each day. Frank, I promise I'll treat you to lunch at Gneeezles to make up for all of this…uh, on second thought, maybe we'll go somewhere else where the food won't choke us and shatter our teeth.

I salute my beloved sister and partner in crime, Sandi Solá, who at one time harbored a certain white-and-black terrier—the actual feisty, seventeen-pound Chihuahua-terrier Jack Russell-lookalike Gneeecey, whom I understand never paid her a dime in rent.

Sooperflea (my sleek black beagle-terrier, a true superhero who understood words when we spelled them out) and dopey-but-beautiful golden beagle-terrier Flubbubb also continue to be inspirations, as well as my black-and-white high jumping mouse Altitude.

My heart breaks as I write here about my precious "Beagley-Germy Shepherd" Horsey Cookie who passed peacefully in my arms on January 10th, 2019. I consider myself to be a wordsmith, but cannot find words that truly convey my deep love for her and the unconditional love she returned throughout the twelve years we were blessed to have together. She and my other furry babies continue to inspire me, from heaven.

I'd be remiss not to thank Nicki Rodriguez, my alter ego, for always showing up and never being at a loss for words.

Guess I'm supposed to say something regarding this book's unsolicited foreword forced upon me by Gneeecey. Something. There. I said it.

And many thanks, of course, to the fine citizens of both HyenaZitania and Perswayssick County, for their (sort of) goodwill and cooperation.

—Vicki Solá
"Regular" New Jersey
January 22, 2019

ENDORSEMENTS

"Get ready for another trip into the wild world created by Vicki Solá. If you enjoyed *The Getaway That Got Away*, you'll love her newest book even more!

—Judy DeAngelis

"If you thought that Solá's wacky aliens couldn't get any funnier, guess again! Just when Nicki thought she had everything back to normal, reality gets a whole new dimension, and we're off again!"

—J. Salter, The 100 Most Influential People Who Never Lived (coauthor)

"Humanoid dog, parallel universe, multi-dimensions; the world, sometimes frantic action and humor of author Vicki Solá, is a delightful read. Her fantasy, use of dialogue, and fresh narrative make the fantastic seem like walking the dog in the park; if by dog, you mean thoroughly untrained humanoid dog with a sassy mouth; and if by park, you mean multi-dimensional chaos; and if by walk, you mean travel with no obvious way home. As you begin this read, be prepared to be hyper-expressingly unpertiminadated."

—Steven Swank (who does many things, author The Horse Knows and Unfold: Selected Poems, 2014-2016, and www.creativeimperatives.com)

Made in the USA
Middletown, DE
12 April 2019